NOIR

NOIR

Robert Coover

OVERLOOK DUCKWORTH

NEW YORK • LONDON

This edition first published in hardcover in the United States in 2010 by
Overlook Duckworth, Peter Mayer Publishers, Inc.
New York • London

NEW YORK:
141 Wooster Street
New York, NY 10012

LONDON:
90-93 Cowcross Street
London EC1M 6BF
inquiries@duckworth-publishers.co.uk
www.ducknet.co.uk

Cataloging-in-Publication Data is available from the Library of Congress

Book design and typeformatting by Bernard Schleifer
Manufactured in the United States of America
FIRST EDITION
1 2 3 4 5 6 7 8 9 10
ISBN 978-1-59020-294-4 US
ISBN 978-0-71563-907-8 UK

For Bernard Hoepffner, partner in crime.

NOIR

YOU ARE AT THE MORGUE. WHERE THE LIGHT IS WEIRD. Shadowless, but like a negative, as though the light itself were shadow turned inside out. The stiffs are out of sight, temporarily archived in drawers like meaty data, chilled to their own bloodless temperature. Their stories have not ended, only their own readings of them. In your line of work, this is not a place where things end so much as a place where they begin. Following the usual preamble: You were in your office late. The phone call came in. You pulled on your old trenchcoat with the torn pockets, holstered your heater under your armpit, and headed for the docklands. The scene of the crime. Nightmarishly dark as it usually is down there, even in the middle of most days, lit only by dull swinging streetlamps, the reflective wet streets more luminous than the lamps themselves, though casting no light of their own. Everything shut up tight but as though harboring unspeakable doings behind the locked doors and barred windows. Fishy smell in the air. Black water lapped the concrete landings and wooden piers somewhere down below. Occasional gull honks: pale sea crows, scavenging. Usual small gathering of gawkers, drunks, cops, bums, their faces shadowed by caps and hats. A perverse and sinister lot. Also scavenging. You shouldered your way through them, hands in your coat pockets. But you were too late. The body had already been removed to the morgue. There was only a clumsy chalk drawing on the damp stones, a red patch at the crotch crudely gendering the drawing. Blue was there. As expected. His beat. What are you doing here? he asked. Just out for a stroll, Blue. Captain Blue to you, asshole. Mr. Asshole to you, Blue; she was a client of mine. Who was? You shrugged and lit a cigarette. The body? The killer? The tipster? No idea. The only connection you were sure of was the phone call. Down below you could see a ferry, backed up against the docks, its carport gaping. Which was disturbing. Could have been anyone. From anywhere. Have to check the passenger list. If there was any. It means things will be messy.

Now, at the morgue, the night attendant tells you a body was brought in, but it's gone again. Must have got stolen, he says. How the fuck could it have been stolen, Creep? Don't know, man. I been here all night.

It was here and then it wasn't here, what can I say. You slap him around a bit to remind him of the hazards of losing a body and ask him what she looked like.

Medium tall, well stacked, painted toenails but not much makeup, no jewelry, blondish hair, same color as her pussy.

She was naked?

Not when she came in.

Where are her clothes?

They're gone, too. Except for this. He hands you a gossamery black veil. You recognize it. Or think you do. You pocket it and turn to leave.

One more thing, the Creep says. You turn back. Her pussy, he says, stroking himself. You can see the sparkle in his buggy little eyes.

Yeah?

Creamy. Soft. Like wet velvet.

IT WAS LATE AFTERNOON WHEN SHE FIRST TURNED UP AT your office. Blanche had left for the day. Which was fading, the lights dim. Maybe she planned it that way, entering as though bringing on the night. Or dragging it in in her wake. She was dressed in black widow's weeds, her face veiled. You'd seen her type before. But there was something about her. A looker, sure, but more than that. A kind of presence. She was poised, cool, yet somehow vulnerable. Tough but tender. It might just be a social call, you thought, taking your feet off your desk and lowering them into the puddled shadows on the floor. Or she could be hiding a murder, fearing one, plotting one. Fearing one, was what she said. Her own. She wanted you to tail a certain person. She handed you a piece of paper with a name on it. You tried not to wince. Mister Big. How did you get mixed up with this guy? you asked.

He was a business partner of my late husband.

Why late? What happened to him?

I don't know. I thought you could find out. The verdict was suicide.

But you think it might have been murder, you said. She sat, lowered her head. A nod perhaps. That's what you took it for. It won't be easy, you thought. The man is protected by an army of thugs and is said to have half a dozen lookalike doubles moving about the city as decoys. Though who these were was hard to say because no one knew what he looked like in the first place.

The widow seemed to be studying her pale hands, fingers laced together in her black lap. You did likewise, studied her hooks: sensuous expressive mitts of a dame in her thirties, unaccustomed to hard work, ornamented only by a wedding ring. With a big rock. Why she wasn't wearing gloves. No sign of nervousness or uncertainty. She knew what she was doing, whatever it was.

She looked like trouble and the smart thing probably would have been to send her packing. But the rent has to be paid, you don't have enough business to turn down anyone. And besides, you liked her legs. So, instead, even though you knew her story before you heard it, the inevitable chronicle of sex, money, betrayal (what the fuck is the matter with the world anyway?), you asked her to tell it. From the beginning, you said.

I AM NOT FROM THE CITY. MY EARLY YEARS WERE SPENT in a small country town far from here, a pretty village with neat tree-lined streets, well-kept lawns, schools and churches that were right in the neighborhood, and a sunny central park with a white wooden bandstand where bands played on weekends. A town where everybody knew each other and loved each other and said hello to each other on the streets and no one was afraid. What I remember now was how much light there was. My father was the town pharmacist and taught Sunday school at church; my mother held bridge parties and volunteered in the municipal library. I was a drum majorette and my younger brother, a happy-go-lucky boy, played on the school basketball team. We were very happy. I was in love with the captain of the school football team and he was in love with me. But then one day my father caught us in what he mistakenly thought were compromising circumstances, and in a fit of temper he sent me away from home. I was only sixteen years old and penniless and all alone in the world when I arrived here in the city. I was, as you can imagine, utterly bereft and desolate, overwhelmed by grief and despair, and facing the hard realities of poverty and loneliness with fear in my heart. But then, by the happiest stroke of good fortune, the sort I thought was never to be mine again, I was able to obtain a position as a maid in the house of the kind and generous man who was later, after the death of his beautiful wife, whom he loved dearly and whose death nearly brought on his own, to become my husband. I tended his critically ill wife through her final days, while he wept at her bedside. The poor man was shattered when she died and became bedridden himself and I had to care for him, too. An affection grew up between us and in time we married. And that is my whole story, except for my husband's tragic and mysterious death which has brought me here this evening.

SHE REACHED UNDER HER BLACK VEIL IN THE DARKENING office (outside, the neon light was doing its nightly stuttering-heartbeat turn) and dabbed at her eyes with a white lace handkerchief. Until she did that, you believed her story because you had no reason not to. Now, it seemed as full of holes as her black veil. You had a hundred questions to ask, but with a silky whisper she crossed her legs and you forgot them. So instead you told her it was a tough assignment, you'd need to buy some help, there would have to be some dough up front.

She uncrossed her legs (you thought you saw sparks) and reached into her purse, handed you a fat bankroll. No need to count it. I'm sure you will find it adequate. It was more lettuce than you'd seen outside the salad bar at Loui's, but you tossed it dismissively on your desk, lit a cigarette and, sending some smoke her way like a searching inquiry (or maybe just, vicariously, to feel her up), said you'd see what you could do.

She stood to go, batting at the smoke. What does the M stand for, Mr. Noir? she asked, nodding toward the sign painted on the street window behind you, seen in reverse from in here: PHILIP M. NOIR / PRIVATE INVESTIGATIONS.

Family name, you said. She thought about that for a moment, then she moved toward the door, nylons whistling softly as though through lips not fully puck-ered. You remembered one of the forgotten questions and, while she was standing in the doorway, silhouet-ted against the hanging hallway bulb outside, you asked it: You said you were caught by your old man in compromising circumstances . . . ?

Yes, well . . . we were not wearing any clothes. But it was completely innocent. We were young and curious.

We've all been there, you said, trying to imagine the scene. But where—?

Oh, on the bandstand, if you must know. On a Sunday afternoon. We intended to collect money after-wards. For charity. A childish idea, I know . . .

THAT NIGHT, IN CELEBRATION OF YOUR NEW CASE, YOU decided to treat yourself to a steak dinner at Loui's Lounge. But before you went, you pocketed your .22 and dropped down to the docklands to look up an alley merchant named Rats, who was always good for a tip or two, even on occasion a reliable one. This time, instead of having to muscle it out of him, you had some scratch to lay on him. A desolate part of town, busy enough by day, but a grim warren of crime and human misery by night. A few lowlife gin mills, some illegal backstreet gambling joints, a couple of flophouses, and a lot of ominously dark streets. The bodies on the sidewalks could be bums or drunks, could be corpses. You recognized one of Rats' runners lurking in an alleyway and told the kid you wanted to see the man. You gave the kid a bill to authenticate your request, then backed into a shadowy doorway, your hand in your pocket gripping your rod, eyes scanning the wet night streets for trouble. A couple of blocks away you saw a pair of cops silhouetted against the ghostly backdrop of the sky-blue police building behind them, yapping with a prostitute. Propositioning her maybe, or pumping her for info. Or just hassling her because they got their kicks that way.

Someone was watching you. And then they weren't. You lit up. Whereupon Rats emerged warily out of the shadows. A scrawny unshaven grifter with a short gimpy leg, paranoid eyes, and a permanent sneer, carved there with a knife. It's the kind of face you'd be wearing if your face read the way you felt about the way things were. You offered him a smoke, passed him a bill, big enough for merchandise as well as info. You realized that one of the questions you'd forgot to ask the dame was her name and the name of her dead husband. But you described her visit to your office and Rats knew who you were talking about, he had also noticed her legs (in the news shots, he said), and he filled you in. They say her gent offed himself, but she reckons he was rubbed out, Rats. What have you heard? He shrugged. They found him with a hole in his head, he said, and a .38 in his hand. Registered to him. No other prints. You nodded, took a drag. Cut and dried, hunh? He dropped his butt to the damp pavement and ground it out with the three-inch heel he wears on his right boot to keep him from tipping sideways. Not quite, he said, releasing the smoke like a kept secret. The hole was in the yoyo's right temple. The gun in his left hand.

RATS, YOU'RE THINKING TONIGHT, MIGHT KNOW SOMEthing about the missing body, having a market interest in them. And about why your pal Fingers got hit last night and by whom. After paying your respects at the Woodshed by lifting a glass or two and asking a few questions, you drop back down to the docks, but no sign of the dealer or his runners. The car ferry has pulled out. The dark streets are empty, or seemingly empty. There is always a restless scurry in them that might or might not be partly human. The chalk drawing is still there, but it has changed since yesterday. The figure is on its side now, head to knees. And something has been added. Outrage is not generally in your repertoire of emotions. You've seen too much, taken too many hard hits, expect the worst as a matter of course. But sometimes your repertoire expands. Like now. You want to thump somebody. Terminally.

You head on down to Skipper's Waterfront Saloon, a smoky lowlife dive the cops call the Dead End Café, they've hauled so many stiffs out of there. Skipper's a cantankerous old seadog with a heavy limp, his face mapped by ropy scars, a dead-black patch over one eye like the opening of a tunnel into the void. The last thing some men see, it's said. Telling their future. Everybody's future. Skipper rarely talks, just lets things be known. He points to his black patch. He points to you. Lets his parrot do all the talking. Hit me again, baby, it says. Squawk! Hit me where it hurts. Whores, mostly well past their prime, ply their trade freely in here, Skipper taking his cut by way of the room he rents them by the halfhour at the back. A filthy vermin-infested and foul-smelling hole in the wall with stained unwashed sheets, shadeless bedside lamp on the floor beside the mattress, the bulb painted red, used hypo spikes underfoot, a basin and pitcher for douches. You know. You've been there.

Romance. Comes all ways.

The smoke in here is thick enough to slice and sell as sandwich meat. You light up in self-defense, order a double, straight up, no ice, ask about Rats. He's on holiday, you're told. Meaning he has been sent up or is on the lam. Blue's here, though. Duty or picking up a piece of the action, who can say. He comes over and says: I thought I told you to steer clear of here, buttbrain.

How can I? It's my second home. If you give me a minute I'll think of my first.

Don't be stupid. You can get badly fucked over in this neighborhood.

I was hoping you'd protect me, officer.

Don't kid yourself, Noir. I look forward to chalking your final portrait.

Speaking of that, what happened to the artwork out in the street? Yesterday it showed a figure with its arms and legs sprawled out. Now it's curled up on its side. And there's the dog . . .

Homicide's been here. Maybe they saw things differently.

They saw a dead dog fucking a dead woman? How come we missed that?

Just not paying attention, I guess.

You've got a problem, Blue. Not just who killed the woman, but who killed the dog? And what was the weapon, by the way?

I give up. Sexual ecstasy?

You feel like belting him one, but his goons would make your night even more unpleasant than it already is, so instead you show him the piece of paper the dame gave you. What does this mean? What does this guy have to do with it?

Blue whistles softly. Where'd you get this?

He reaches for it, but you pocket it. It's a kind of talisman. The only physical proof you ever knew the lady; the veil in your pocket may or may not be hers. Picked it up on the street, you say and down your drink, turn to leave. You catch a glimpse of Blue nodding to a couple of his off-duty cops and you figure you're about to get tailed. Or nailed.

Go for it, scumsucker, the parrot squawks. My ass is your ass!

At the door, Michiko, one of the local whores, comes over to flirt with you. Hey, Phil-san, she whispers, wrapping her parchmenty arms around your neck. She uses a body powder that makes you think of an airless hothouse. She looks like she is dressed from head to toe in a densely patterned body stocking, but she is actually wearing only her skin and a thong—if that's not a tattoo, too. She leans close to your ear as though to nibble at it and whispers: Go out back door, Phil-san. Somebody waiting for you in front. C'mon, baby, she says more loudly, reaching into your pants. Quickie-quickie? Michiko love you!

⊙

MICHIKO WAS NOT ALWAYS A SUFFOCATINGLY PERFUMED bag of old painted bones. She had a certain enigmatic Eastern aura when she was younger and worked the snazzier joints. Before that, while she was still just a kid in schoolgirl clothes and white cotton panties (white panties used to be a big deal; you miss those times), she had been the moll of a notorious yakuza gangster who had his own portrait tattooed on the inside of her tender young thighs. Where he could keep an eye on things, he said. A rival gang leader kidnapped her and "blinded" the portrait with red splotches, and just for good measure added a mustache and blacked out two of the teeth before returning her to her lover. He also had his own hand, recognizable by its don't-fuck-with-me dragon tattoo on the back and the superhero code ring on his pinkie, tattooed over her plucked pubes, the middle finger disappearing between her lips. Her lover responded by sending her back to the rival with the dragon tattoo reduced to a simpering please-fuck-me position, the ring finger chopped to a bloody stub, signifying a humiliating three-knuckled yubizume, and the middle finger blackened as though torched by its impertinence. The lover also tattooed Michiko's ears with haikus celebrating the "black mist" of summer and winter's "ice-heart," which was a play on his own name, and inked the circles of a target on her buttocks around the bull's-eye anus with the phrase "You're next, asshole!" on the right cheek. The rival was not dismayed. With a simple stroke he changed winter's "ice-heart" to winter's "withered-dick," which also turned out to be a play on the lover's name, assumed the "asshole" could be either of them and so merely added a semiautomatic weapon on her left cheek with his gang's insignia on the handle. On her face, he tattooed a snake, the head coiling out of one ear onto Michiko's upper lip, its mouth biting its own tail, which was coiling out of the other ear, the face of the snake a portrait of the lover, the tail the lover's own cock, which was famously (a favorite subject of the tabloids) tattooed with the Kanji symbols for "King of Water Business." This the rival subtly altered to "King of Urine Business" and sent her back again. The lover accepted the biting snake, but put a face on the bitten tail with very big ears, mocking the rival's donkey ears which he always tried to keep pinned under his black fedora ("Mister Hee Haw" is what the cops called him, and they loved to humiliate him by knocking his hat off), and applying the Kanji symbols for "Number One Hot-Ass Warrior" to the head. Then, just for fun (he loved her after all and wished her to be beautiful) he turned her breasts into magnificent mountainous landscapes with little bridges over streams that his own gang members posed on in their pinstriped suits, holding up placards that read: Do not dream mountains from anthills, pisant. The scene invited interpolations and the rival obliged by turning it into a classic yakuza bloodbath with his own gang, disguised as giant ants in black fedoras and suits, wiping out the lover's gang. He decorated her belly with a bulbous raccoon-dog with testicles like beach balls, etched a crimson "4" on her forehead, the sign of death, inscribed a stormy seascape on her backside with giant waves crashing over the small of her back, and converted the target into a whirlpool with a fishing boat being dragged down into its dark center, giving one the sense, if one approached her from that direction, of entering the eye of the storm. Thus, she continued to get passed back and forth between the two yakuza bosses as a kind of message board, the gangsters coming to so admire each other's art in the end that their rivalry, to the disgust of all their gang members, became purely an artistic epistolary one. They covered her with fragments of famous scenic and erotic masterpieces, always with implicit or explicit threats and insults, burned the signs of the zodiac in the appropriate places on her body, inscribed four centuries of yakuza history in all the blank spaces, covering even the soles of her feet, her lips and scalp, her eyelids and armpits. So obsessed were they, they might have started working on her insides had not their own lieutenants organized a public exhibit of Michiko in the city's modern art museum and, at the moment that they bowed to one another, executed both of them with tattoo needles fired into their ears. Michiko meanwhile ended up tattooed from crown to toes with layers of exotic overwritten graffiti, a veritable yakuza textbook, slang dictionary, and art gallery, a condition that served her well in her subsequent career, once the museum, which claimed ownership of her, was paid off: she was worth a C-note just for an hour of library time. All of it fading now. Losing its contours, its clarity, the colors muddying, wrinkles disturbing the continuities, obscuring the detail. Suffering the fate of all history, which is only corruptible memory. Time passes, nothing stays the same; a sad thing. A haiku somewhere on her body says as much.

AT THE BACK DOOR, MICHIKO PLEADS SOFTLY: COME see me, baby, Michiko fuck your ears off! and hands you a folded piece of paper. You kiss the yellowing "4" on her forehead (up yours, death), pat her picturesque patoot and slip away into the dark hollow night. Foghorn somewhere. A cat's anguished howl. As if expressing your grief for you. You find a lone streetlamp by which to read the note, but you hear Michiko scream and then running footsteps. Coming your way. You duck down an alleyway, scale the brick wall at the end, jump down into somebody's back garden on the other side. There's a lonely woman undressing in a window, silhouetted against a drawn blind. On the other side of that blind lies another story, better maybe than the one you're in and one you might reasonably pause to explore as a kind of intriguing sidebar, but first, by the light of the window, you read the note Michiko passed you. It says: Urgent. See me at Loui's. No signature. The handwriting could be Flame's. On the other hand, you've never seen Flame's handwriting. You play out the story behind the blind in your mind and, as the silhouetted woman lifts her slip over her head, hurry on down the glittering night street toward Loui's Lounge.

Loui, or Louis (you've never known for sure if Loui was his name or if that was a neon typo, but everyone calls him Loui) is a pal of yours. You helped him duck an assault and battery rap brought against him by his latest ex by uncovering some dirt about her she didn't want brought out in court. To wit, that she was a klepto and aggressively into shoplifting, if the bigtime moves she made (she could strip out whole stores right under the owners' noses) could still be called that. You didn't tell him how you found out, he wouldn't have liked that part. The mob likes to eat here and for some obscure reason, maybe just happy bellies, they have taken Loui into their confidence, with the consequence that he is, indirectly, a source of useful dope about them. He knows if he gives anything away he will be executed in a cruel manner and buried in concrete at the bottom of the sea, and in his anxiety not to reveal what he knows he invents elaborate disinformation of his own, which with patience can usually be decoded. His lounge is an upscale joint with underdressed hatcheck girls, aged whiskeys, live torchers who mix with the clientele, slots in the back room, and prime rib on the menu. The cocktail napkins use the motif of a drunk in a tux, leaning against a lamp post, and the clock over the bar repeats it, the drunk's arms as the clock's hands. Happy hour starts at 5:45 when the minute hand rises to a full erection.

You chase off the wimp who's sitting on your customary stool at the bar and order up a double on the rocks, ice being potable in this hole. Joe the bartender, wearing a poker face, greets you as he would a stranger, which probably means that something's up. Flame is in the middle of a song about a brutal lover called the Hammer (there are rhymes like wham her, jam her, slam her, and goddamn her), who can be lethal (. . . *I know you think you're the big cheese, but, baby, don't kill me, please,* she sings), and you expect her to drop over after her number, but before that a big-fisted suit sits down on the stool beside you and offers to buy you a drink and you realize things are not as you thought. I've got one, you say. Have another, he says and signals the bartender. Beware of geeks bearing gifts, you say, and pull your glass back. Suit yourself, he says with a shrug and taps his own glass for a refill. Just trying to have a friendly conversation, mac. What about? You're looking for a body, he says. Yeah? Stop looking. The Hammer is ramming: *It's just a little trick,* Flame sings, *but it's got a mean kick.* . . . You can see that the suit has a gat pointed at you from his jacket pocket. You'd be dead before you reached your own. You set your glass back on the bar and shrug at Joe. If you insist, you say dryly.

Before Joe can pour, the song ends and Flame comes over and interposes herself between the two of you. Move your ass, buster. I want to converse with my lover here. Joe is also coldly staring him down. The suit scowls but takes his hand out of his pocket and slips back into the shadows. Flame kisses you, running her tongue along your teeth as if checking to see if the ones that remain are all still there, then nibbles at your ear, pressing up between your legs. Looks like you're staying here tonight, lover, she whispers. Her wild-animal aroma is dizzying. Who does that bozo work for? you ask, stroking Flame's silky backside. You know, she says. Over her shoulder you can see Loui's bouncers disarm the suit and toss him. Why did you come here tonight, Phil? After what happened to Fingers, you must've known there'd be trouble. They know you were at the Shed last night. I got a note, sweetheart. I thought it was from you. If I want you here, baby, I don't have to write a note. I just send out vibes. This is true. You often turn up here on what you call intuition and find her waiting for you, her desire like a magnet. Not for nothing does she call her lovers moths.

YOU MET FLAME THE NIGHT THE RICH WIDOW FIRST BANK-rolled you and you went out to celebrate, figuring on oysters and prime rib at Loui's. Maybe pick up a lead or two, as often happens, like a side dish on the menu. Rats had filled you in on the basics of the case down by the docks, and laid some class blow on you to boot, so when you arrived your mood was definitely upbeat. You greeted Joe and Loui effusively like long lost brothers (if you have any brothers, they are certainly long lost), tucked some bills in the cleavages of the hatcheck girls, and bought drinks for everybody. Including yourself. But then you set yours down and forgot where and had to buy another and made it another round. You were having a good time. All the while you were watching Loui's new redheaded torch singer, aglow under the spotlight like a hallucination. A smoky voice and the sort of body that cracks mirrors. Last time you saw a body like that was in a wet dream

when you were still in knee pants, and because you did-
n't know what to do, it was more like a nightmare.
Now you knew what to do. As you were, being
momentarily flush, a big spender on the night, she was
naturally watching you, too. She was singing a song
asking longingly for an old lover named Charlie who
was always good to her: you flashed your stash at her
to lure her over after her set. Loui, standing at the bar
with you, introduced you to each other (Philip is a private dick, Flame, he told her, hard but doting . . .), and
then, after Flame leaned down and kissed his bald pate,
waddled off table-hopping, greeting his customers.
What's your real name, sweetheart, you asked her, ever
the tireless investigator.

Well, the one before Flame was Fannie, if that's
what you mean, but using it was just an invitation to
pinch it. Men can't seem to stop themselves, she said,
wincing (you couldn't stop yourself). She parted the
satiny curtains of her long split skirt and peeled her silken
undies down off one hip to show you the bruises. Kiss
them, honey, to make them well, she said and you did.

She asked you where all the lucre came from and
you told her about the rich widow and related the story
she told you.

Not many jobs in town for drum majorettes,
she said. She probably had to work the streets. So she
meets this rich john . . .

In short, Flame was soon burning holes in the widow's story. You showed her the note she'd given you. Flame whistled softly. Looks like your last night as a nobody, Phil. Let's go to my room and have a group snuggle, you, me, and Charlie.

I was planning on dinner.

Have Loui bring it to you. Get the Big Guy Special, we can share it. Come on. Once those yobs know what you're up to, we may never get another chance. A chilling thought. Shriveled you right up. Fortunately Flame was able to do something about that with her little deicer.

$\odot$

YOUR SECRETARY BLANCHE ALSO HAD HER DOUBTS ABOUT the widow's story when you told it to her the next morning. Blanche is a born skeptic. She can never just accept the world at face value. Which is admittedly somewhat less than nada, a bad investment. And Blanche always starts with the money: Did she pay you anything?

A little.

By the looks of you this morning, Mr. Noir, it was more than enough.

Well, I think she liked me.

Don't be naïve, she said, giving you a scolding

look over the top of her horn-rimmed glasses. It was a business transaction. She expects to get all that back and more.

Maybe the dame just wanted to save her ass, Blanche, pardon the French. She said she was afraid she might be knocked off and asked me to tail a guy.

Who? You showed her the slip of paper with Mister Big's name on it. Oh oh. What does this gentleman have to do with it?

He was her dead husband's business partner.

So they are both going after the same money. That's why she's afraid. Or he is. Must be something wrong about the insurance policy. A no-suicide clause or something. Or else the will. Was there a will?

She didn't say.

You didn't ask. Blanche sighed impatiently, tapping her pencil against her teeth. I'll call my friend at the Registry, see what I can find out.

Thanks. What would I do without you, kid?

She seemed to melt momentarily, then quickly turned brisk again, jotting down some notes. You can't type and have no head for numbers and only insult people when they call on the blower, so you rely utterly on Blanche, her irritating superciliousness the price you pay. A no-nonsense blonde, not much fun, but she can count and sort and sponge up the daily trivia. Empty the wastebaskets. She does not always come in to the office, you never know when to expect her, but you can't pay her anything except compliments, so you can't complain.

Whose money was this in the first place? she asked, studying her notes.

You mean, the husband's?

I mean, whose *really*? My guess is it belonged to the dying wife. What did she die of?

I didn't ask about that either. Do you think it's important?

Think, Mr. Noir, think. You said your client's father was a pharmacist.

Right. And taught Sunday school.

And the wife, you said, died a lingering death. A man wants to get rid of a wealthy wife in a discreet manner and meets a woman with access to pharmaceuticals.

Hmm. But she and her father aren't speaking. He threw her out of the house.

She said. For exposing herself in a lewd manner in the town park. Not long after Sunday School.

Yes. He was outraged.

Or jealous.

Oh my God, Blanche. You have a really evil imagination.

Just a practical one, Mr. Noir. You could use a bit of the same. It might help you to stop associating with wicked and dangerous persons. Whatever made you take up this case?

Well, she has nice legs.

Legs are legs, Mr. Noir. There are more of them than there are people.

Sure, but—

And a bullet in the brain is a bullet in the brain. As her husband could tell you, were it not too late.

⊙

WHILE BLANCHE CHASED DOWN THE WILL AND INSURance policy, you stretched out on the office sofa to think things out. You seemed to be following clues that led nowhere. Which became the pursuit of a criminal with five legs, only three of them human. When you woke up it was dark and you didn't know where you were. The blinking neon light outside the window, however, was a useful hint. It had a short and made a stuttery buzzing sound like bugs hitting an electric screen. Electrocution. Pest control. Once you woke up in an electrocution chamber. This was a different case. A member of the mob who was electrocuted for murder later turned up on the streets. About that same time, the warden left for Brazil. The hood killed some people but they said he couldn't be prosecuted because he was already dead. A double? Or funny business at the death house? A rival mobster hired you to find out. You snuck in to check the circuits. Hit the wrong wire.

So, alone in your darkened office, that's where you were. Where you feel most at home. You have a bedsit somewhere, but mostly you eat and sleep here when you're not being entertained by some dame. It's a place where you can pick your nose, scratch your itches, fart your farts. Which, on the occasion, stretched out there in the dark after a daylong nap, you did. You lifted your butt off the cushions and let fly. That's better, you said aloud.

I'm sure it is.

You were not alone. There was someone sitting in the shadows. Your client, the generous widow. You didn't know whether to apologize, let another, or change the subject. Tell me about your father, you said.

Well, that's what I came to talk about, Mr. Noir. There was something I didn't tell you. Although my father was a loving father who doted on my mother, my brother, and me, he could be hard on us when we misbehaved. Like many in our little town, he had a rather pure Biblical notion of obedience, which was sometimes difficult for us to live up to. I was his favorite and fared better than my brother who was, I must say, quite terrified of him. And as we were obliged to witness each other's punishment as a kind of deterrent, I quite understood his terror and, on his behalf, shared it. But after you received your due and thanked him for it, he was always forgiving and hugged you tenderly to his bosom and gave you candy from the drugstore, making you promise not to disappoint him again. But of course we always did. In the town park, they sold popcorn and cotton candy on Sundays; he often took us there, it was so nice. And one day, when I was a little girl, walking past the wooden bandstand with him, I saw a thin pale rubbery thing like a dead worm. Or, rather, what appeared to be the empty skin of a worm like the skins molted by snakes. I let go his hand and reached down and picked it up, and my father slapped it fiercely out of my hands and smacked the side of my head so hard I flew against the side of the bandstand. When the tears flowed, he cuddled me and apologized and promised to show me a clean one and what they were really for. And it turned out they were in fact a little as I had imagined.

Aha. I have it, you said. When he threw you out, it was not out of righteous anger. He was jealous. Your father was your first lover.

Of course not! You have an evil imagination, Mr. Noir!

Not really. I just borrowed it.

You sat up and yawned and tapped out a fag. And your brother?

But she was gone. You worried you'd just lost another client. But there was another roll of bills on your desk, with the note: *Are you protecting me, Mr. Noir?*

YOU WERE NOT. IT WAS TIME TO FACE UP TO MISTER BIG. But if you found him, tailed him, uncovered a plot, what? No way to reach the widow, you'd failed to ask for an address or phone number. Your notorious impatience with details. It's why you need Blanche. Rats had told you her name, you'd paid him for it, but you had forgotten it. All you could remember was the butt ground under Rats' three-inch heel and Flame's deicer. That kind of night.

You phoned your pal Snark, your inside feed in Blue's unit, and asked him to meet you at the Star Diner. The Diner doesn't have a liquor license, but for those in the know, they keep whiskey in the milk dispenser. Snark is a heavy drinker and usually after five or six mugfuls he starts opening up. The trick is to keep up with him. Waiting for him, you ordered up a bowl of chili, a fresh doughnut, and a mug of black coffee. If pressed, you'd have to admit you prefer the cooking in here to the fancy spread at Loui's. You'd just got paid. You could have two doughnuts. One of them jelly-filled.

Another of Snark's soft spots, you could share it with him. He likes to dip them in his whiskey. You also ordered up several glasses of ice water and put them down as fortification for the night ahead.

When he arrived, you got him jawing about his family, station gossip (Blue was suffering a violent case of redhot hemorrhoids and was making life hell for everyone), tips on the horses, and recent crimes, mostly of the gory sort, Snark's particular métier. Snark has an unusual family. A pair of Siamese twins for kids and a wife who's a professional contortionist. She was working up an nightclub act with the twins that Snark said he hoped would be big enough to allow him to retire from the force. When he's tanked enough, Snark will describe all the positions his wife can get into. Snark himself can't touch his toes, even with his knees bent.

After a few (it was getting ugly, he was talking about the positions the twins could get into), you told him the widow's tale and showed him the piece of paper.

That's deep shit, he said, and took another slug from his mug of whiskey. Outside, an old panhandler with long white hair and beard was pressing his bulbous nose against the window, gazing hauntingly in upon your conversation. You'd often seen him out there, he was part of the scenery in his old weathered topcoat and rumpled fedora, unwashed gray-black clothing held together with frayed sashweight cord. Hunched shoulders, caved-in chest, his limp beard down to his belt, plastic bags full of dustbin debris, a living piece of the inner city. More or less living. He often had something poetical to say, like I got the city inside me, mister, it's weighin' me down and suckin' up all my brain juice, or I seen a bird today with a broken wing and a cat et it and a car hit the cat. Who is this broad? Snark asked.

Her name? I don't know. I learned it and then I unlearned it. You tapped your own whiskey mug in explanation. You realized you'd spotted your tie with the chili. Not the first time. It's why you wear patterned ties. Her husband killed himself. Or was killed.

I think I know the case. He drowned himself. With his feet in concrete.

I think it was a shooting.

Well, maybe he drowned himself, and *then* shot himself. Or vice versa. I'm sure it was him.

What I need to know, Snark, you said, scraping at your tie, is how do I get to Mister Big?

Well, he has a weakness for pedicures.

I don't do toenails.

Also toy soldiers.

Toy soldiers?

Yeah, they tell me his office walls are lined with

glass cases full of them. He dresses up and plays out battles on his billiard table.

Hmm. Any specialty?

Medieval. He digs the Dark Ages.

⊙

WHEN SNARK LEFT, YOU BOUGHT A DOUGHNUT DIPPED IN pink sugar and took it out to the old panhandler. He tipped his crumpled fedora and, staring up at you with watery blue eyes curtained by long strands of dirty white hair, said: They was a woman had a dog that done tricks. The dog got sick and died and the woman got sick and died. Don't know which come first. But no one remembers the tricks the dog done. Just me. If you ever need to know, mister, just ask me. He put the pink doughnut in one of his plastic bags and shuffled away. Was he going to eat the doughnut? Sell it? Bury it? Where was he going? What else was in his bags? On a hunch, you followed him. What were you thinking? That he might reveal something about the city that you didn't know. Something that would be a kind of clue. On the principle that opposites attract, you thought, he might even lead you to Mister Big. Why not. Besides, you were restless. You'd slept all day, drunk too much, needed to walk it off. Snark was heavy duty.

The old panhandler's route was a twisty one down bleak abandoned streets, ever narrower, darker, and more labyrinthine. A wind was blowing down them, chasing scraps of rag and newspaper, causing signs and hanging lamps to squeal and sway. Sometimes all you could see were the blown newspapers and the panhandler's long white hair and beard flowing along in the shadows. There seemed no pattern to his wanderings, though he stopped at each trashbin and poked around, so maybe he was making his nightly rounds. Doing his collections, straightening up the city, he the only feeble sign of life within it. You'd been trailing along and no longer knew where you were. Didn't matter. Though you wished you'd remembered to pack heat, you were at home nowhere and anywhere. And there was something about these dark nameless streets going nowhere that resonated with your inner being. The desolation. The bitterness. The repugnant underbelly of existence. Well, you'd eaten too fast. The doughnuts and chili hadn't settled well. As the old fellow stooped over some gutter refuse, you stepped into a doorway, cupped your hands around a struck match, lit up. You smelled something familiar. And then the lights went out.

THE CITY AS BELLYACHE. THE URBAN NIGHTMARE AS AN expression of the vile bleak life of the inner organs. The sinister rumblings of the gut. Why we build cities the way we do. Why we love them the way they are even when they're dirty. *Because* they're dirty. Pissed upon, spat upon. Meaningless and deadly. We can relate to that. Here's a principle: The body is always sick. Even when it's well, or thinks it is. Cells are eating cells. It's all about digestion. Or indigestion. What in the city we call corruption. Eaters eating the eaten. Mostly in the tumultuous dark. It's a nasty fight to the finish and everybody loses. Cities laid out on grids? The grid's just an overlay. Like graph paper. The city itself, inside, is all roiling loops and curves. Bubbling with a violent emptiness. You have often pondered this, especially after suppers at the Star Diner. You were pondering it that night when some semblance of consciousness returned. Pondering is not the word. Your buffeted mind, its shell sapped, was incapable of pondering. It was more like an imageless dream about pain and the city. Almost imageless. You were being dragged through an old film projector. Your mazy crime-ridden gut was on view somewhere. Your sprocket holes were catching, tearing. Your head was caught in the mechanism. Fade out.

⊙

BEFORE YOU COULD SEE ANYTHING, YOU COULD HEAR water sloshing lazily against stones like crumpling metal. The dirty spatter of rain, squawk of gulls. You were down at the waterfront. They must have dragged you here. You opened one eye. Everything in shades of gray, slick with rain. Could be twilight. Probably dawn. You were lying on your belly on wet rocks and broken concrete under an old iron bridge down in the docklands at dawn. In the rain. Everything hurt. Head felt cracked open. To rise up on one elbow took an heroic effort, but you were a hero. Your clothes were a mess. But your tie had been laundered.

Captain Blue was sitting on an old truck tire in a police slicker and rain hat, smoking a cigarette. He tossed you the pack. It was your own. One left. You fumbled for matches but they were wet. Blue came over irritably (you were wasting his time) and let you light your cigarette off his, then he sat down again. So what are you doing down here, dipshit? he asked. They throw you out of your flophouse?

I had a yearning for the bracing seaside air, you said, and felt your pockets.

You were lucky, Noir. It wasn't robbery. When we found you, you still had your bankroll.

Oh yeah? Where is it?

I shared it out with the guys. Reward for saving your useless fucked-up life.

What do you mean, saving my life? What did they do?

It's what they didn't do. Pretty mean old boys, Noir. Now where did that big roll come from?

Client of mine. At the bottom of an empty pocket, a nearly empty pocket, there was a wrinkled scrap of paper. The name the widow scribbled out for you. You tried to remember that familiar smell you noticed just before they brained you, but your sinuses were clogged now with the odor of dead fish and machine oil.

Don't bullshit me, scumbag, your clients don't have that kinda money. What are you up to?

You sighed. Even that hurt. So the sigh was more like a groan. You'd smoked the cigarette down to the point where it was burning your lips, and you badly needed another. You flicked the tiny fagend toward the water where rotting pilings from collapsed wooden docks reared up out of the greasy water like ancient stalagmites, black bones, and said: Collecting for police charity.

I oughta take you over to the station, wiseass, and work you over just for the pleasure of it. But somebody's already done that for us.

Who do you think that was?

I don't know. My guess is you've picked up a tail.

Is that a guess or inside track?

Educated guess, let's say. Out in the dead black

water, pimpled with rain, rusting barges with angular bent-neck cranes sat like senile old geezers having a mindless bath. You don't know why you notice such things. You're a nosy guy, Noir, Blue said, and nosy guys attract the curiosity of other nosy guys.

Crushed beer cans. An old shoe. Rusting hubcap. Broken crate slats. Piece of sewer pipe. Bent plastic bottles. Debris of the shore, snuggling in the rocks. Integers. Adding up to nothing. Still, you keep on doing the fucking math. You staggered to your feet, feeling like shit. Think I'm going to have to change the mattress, you said.

Snark says there's a woman involved.

Yeah, my mother. She misses me. Take me home to her.

You've got a head wound, numbnuts. You should go to hospital and have it treated, get an X-ray.

An X-ray might break it. I've got work to do.

Your funeral, chump. I don't have a free car, he says, but here. . . . He peeled a tenspot off the roll in his pocket. I'm feeling flush. I'll pay for your cab.

BLANCHE WAS UPSET WHEN SHE SAW THE STATE YOU were in. First thing, get out of those wet clothes, Mr. Noir. You'll catch your death.

I caught it when I got dropped, Blanche. And I don't have any dry ones.

I'll take those things down to the laundromat and put them in the drier. Hurry up now.

You felt like you might pass out. You were making squishy noises when you walked and not just in your shoes. You managed to get your tie off while she was brewing up a cup of tea, but she had to take care of the rest. It was like peeling tinfoil off a cigarette pack. You hoped your shorts weren't dirty. While she was emptying out your pockets, she said: It's that woman you're mixed up with, isn't it? The one with the legs and the fishy story.

Maybe. I think the cops had something to do with it.

She sat you down on a stool and bandaged up your head. This wasn't the first time you'd turned up after a going-over, wouldn't be the last, it was part of the racket, so Blanche always kept a fully stocked body-repair kit in the office. She used up a whole roll of cotton bandage and when she was done your helmeted head bobbed heavily on your shoulders; you felt like lying down but you were afraid of not getting up again. You look like a swami, Mr. Noir, she said, sniffing the wet clothes, then turned to leave.

Wait a minute, Blanche. I can't go around like this. What if someone comes?

She stared at you thoughtfully over her horn-rimmed spectacles, set down the wet clothes, reached under her woolen skirt. Look the other way, Mr. Noir. You sipped at the tea, careful not to tip your head back for fear of it falling off. The tea tasted good; it would have tasted better with something in it, but that was a Blanche no-no. All right, you can look now. You can cover up your unmentionables with these. You'd always thought of Blanche wearing practical white cotton drawers or one of those elastic corsetty things, but what she handed you was a pair of pink silk panties with little flowers stitched on them. The glossy silk felt good but they were a tight fit and some of your unmentionables hung out. She tried to help you push them in, and she could get one side in, but when she tried to push the other side in, the first one popped out. The whole exercise was making you lightheaded.

Leave it, sweetheart. If anyone asks, I'll say I'm airing out my hemorrhoids.

She wasn't gone five minutes, you were still staggering about the room in the tight undies with your head dipping and weaving, fighting the urge to fall out on the sofa, when the widow turned up. Mr. Noir, she said, as though somewhat exasperated. I never know what to expect. Are you really a private detective, or do I have the wrong address?

⊙

YOU'D THINK: LIVE AND LEARN. ONCE BURNED, TWICE shy, all that. If history starts to repeat, you can stop it if you want. Bend it. Or walk away from it. But here you are again in the Star Diner, getting shitfaced from the milk dispenser with Snark after another belly-churning chili-and-doughnut repast, hurting still from last night's waterfront drubbing and breathless from your run from your interrupted railway freight-yard meet with Rats, and listening, while the old white-bearded panhandler peers in from outside, to the newest positions Snark's contortionist wife has treated him to.

Sounds great.

Yeah, except for when she gets so twisted she gets us locked up. Then it can be a long sweaty night.

You nod, trying to imagine this (the contortionist wife is easy enough, but not Snark), and thank him for pulling you out of the drink down at pier four last night. But what was he doing down there?

We were called there on a tip and interrupted a murder. Yours. You were completely out of it but still thrashing away, and by the time we'd got a grip and fished you out, the bozo trying to do you had got away.

The Hammer. There's a body down there. On a yacht.

There are bodies everywhere, Snark says with a certain glum zest, dipping a pistachio-crusted doughnut filled with grape jelly in his whiskey, then putting the whole thing in his mouth. Last night we caught a guy having his old lady for supper, he says, his cheeks bulging with chewed doughnut and oozing purple jelly. She'd been carved up, packaged in butcher's paper, neatly labeled and stored in the refrigerator meat drawer.

Blue stopped by today, Snark. Wants to arrest me for stealing some toy soldiers.

Yeah, I saw him when he left. Expected him to come back with you. Better lay low. He's gunning for you.

He let me go. Not sure why.

Must have thought he could use you somehow.

I think he did. You hit the milk dispenser again. There are a lot of things you want to know but you're here mainly because you thought Snark might know something about the widow and what happened to her body, especially after what Rats just told you about some mystery as to where it was found, the drawing of it. But all Snark is able to tell you is that he thinks goggle-eyes down at the morgue knows something.

The Creep? I already talked to him. He told me she had painted toenails and a blonde snatch. Not much help. Never saw either.

Maybe you should ask him again. And as for bodies down at the docks, listen to the captain. Stay away from there.

The panhandler, his thick nose flattened on the misty window, is gazing in at you soulfully with his watery blue eyes. You start to tell Snark about the night you followed the old fellow and got laid out and, seemingly without transition, you find yourself, as though compelled, following him again, drifting into mazy dimly-lit inner-city streets in the hapless way one drifts into a repeating nightmare. Of course, there has been a transition. You got into a slurry disquisition on the world's inscrutability, how knowing only leads to more unknowing, the world remaining enigmatic, deceptive, dangerous, impenetrable, and Snark, scowling, said, You haven't been messing around with my wife, have you? and lumbered out in a drunken huff, leaving you stuck with the bill. Then the doughnut-and-story routine; you couldn't seem to resist. This time, instead of one dipped in pink sugar, you bought the panhandler a custard-filled chocolate-frosted doughnut, your feeble effort maybe at changing the trajectory. He placed it carefully in one of his plastic bags and said: One day I seen a feller jump offa that building over there. Then I seen it again, a feller jumpin' offa that building. But I don't know if I seen two fellers jumpin' or I seen one feller and then my brain thinkin' about it made two differnt fellers out of it. The next time I thought about it, I seen another feller jumpin'. Or mebbe I seen another feller jumpin' and that made me think of the other ones. The brain's a funny thing, ain't it? So whaddaya think? I seen three fellers jumpin' or I seen just one and my rememberin' brain made me think I seen three?

I think you saw three different guys, you said. I mean, you just thought of it again, didn't you? Did you see a guy jump just now?

Sure. Didn't you?

And then he was shuffling off, you lighting up and, one eye on the rooftops for falling bodies, shuffling along after him, sporting a rod this time, telling yourself that you are trying to figure out what happened last time, who was there in that darkened doorway, but knowing your following is less rational than that. Knowing, in effect, you can't stop yourself.

You know plenty about getting sucked into stories that have already been told. You've used that knowledge in the past to crack a few cases, though usually too late to change anything. And it has happened to you before. This haunting widow is not the first woman to grab you by the nads and drag you into a webby plot not of your own devising. But even if the story's familiar and you know the ending, it's hard to step out of it. Like stepping off a rocketing train. Everybody's on that train. Nobody's an original. To be obsessed is to be a wound-up actor in a conventional melo, with everyone else, the lucky ones, bit players at best. So it's not the story you're trapped in, like everyone else, but, once aware of that, how you play it out. Your style. Class. The moves you make. Steppin' round the beat, as Fingers used to say. How long does that matter? As long as you live. Meaning: no time at all.

Are these twisted nameless streets the same the old panhandler led you down last time? Some corners are familiar, some not. It's as though things have been shifted about or turned around. Different angle maybe. Or maybe just how the inner city works. A way of deflecting and confusing the outsider. The law. The tailing eye. A thin cold rain is falling. You tug your hat brim down over your eyes, avoiding dark doorways, but keeping your eye on them, watching for any movement, cigarette hanging from your lip, the butt of your pocketed .22 gripped in one hand, widow's lacy veil in the other like a lucky charm. You figure you're going to have to plug somebody, that's what the gun in your hand is saying. Insisting upon. The plot-triggering stage prop, another kind of tale entrapment. Old rule of the criminologist: what can happen must happen. Why the planet's fucked. You are more exposed out here in the wet greasy street, but the old panhandler, drifting from shadow to shadow, seems lost in his own trashbin peregrinations, oblivious to the world. You could probably walk alongside him and he wouldn't know you were there. You realize he is not only taking things out, he is also putting things in. A kind of market transaction with the silent bins. If that's what happens to your doughnut, next time you'll only give him half, save the rest for a travel snack. Next time? Hmm. You pause to think about this and (a familiar smell?) the lights go out.

SAME EERILY DESERTED INNER-CITY STREETS, SAME OCCASIONAL streetlamp casting its poor light, same trashbins and shadowy doorways, but everything frozen solid, sheeted with ice. Abandoned tenements, tilting perilously with the weight of their icy crusts, glitter with multiple reflections of the glazed streetlamps, the frozen streets and sidewalks do. There is a faint cracking sound as of the frozen freezing deeper. You can't move and you know, or seem to know, that you are dead. Iced up solid. Unable even to shudder. This knowledge is itself frozen and cannot move on.

YOU'RE PRETTY SURE YOUR EYES ARE OPEN, BUT YOU CAN see nothing. It's like staring into Skipper's eyepatch. The idea that you are dead is still in your head, but the pain there tells you otherwise. And the cold: do the dead feel cold? Is that what hell is? A frozen eternity living with the pain you died with? You start to relax into that in a perverse what-the-fuck way, some treacherous part of your bruised brain telling you to let go— then you catch yourself. Where are you? Some kind of box. A coffin? But cold, like an icebox. And suddenly you know. The crypt at the morgue. The refrigerated vaults. You're in a cadaver drawer.

How do these things work? You can't remember. Your frozen head is throbbing, you can't remember anything. Never been inside a file drawer before though you've opened and closed them often enough. A catch somewhere? You have to stay cool. So to speak. You can't. You're starting to panic. Which means at least you're alive and kicking. Kicking: that's what you're suddenly doing, you're kicking at the far end, recalling now that the stiffs are usually filed head first so one can get idents without having to witness any horrors above the tagged feet or disturb the modesty of the dead. That fucking Creep. If you get out of here, you're going to throttle the evil sonuvabitch with your bare hands. Your desperate kicks are blows to his bug-eyed face. And then there is a metallic snap and light and you're gliding out on steel rollers into the white room, stripped to the frosted buff and wearing a toe tag, about three drawers up.

RATS ONCE TOLD YOU ABOUT A PAL OF HIS WHO DIED whose cadaver got used as a container for a drug shipment. His body was gutted by a friendly mortician with a habit and stuffed with bags of angel dust (snowballs, as Rats calls them) and sewn up again, the brain cavity and scrotum filled with diamonds and emeralds from a recent heist. This was a kind of memorial tribute to his pal, Rats said with his sneering scarfaced grin, the pal, whom he loved like a brother and maybe was a brother, having always referred to his balls as the family jewels. He woulda got a snort outa that. The one mistake they made, Rats said, was not knocking out his pal's gold teeth. Some smalltime hoods got wind of the body in transit, stole it for the teeth, and unaware of the stuffing, threw the remains off an overpass to make it look like suicide. It got struck by a speeding semi, setting off a snowstorm in summer and an orgasmic scatter of jewels that caused a ten-hour traffic jam. Even though all he salvaged from the operation were the two teeth, the cheap hoods soon following his pal off the overpass, and though the mob was on his back for awhile after that, Rats called the failed operation pure poetry, even though it probably wasn't the kind to win a Nobel. Since then, the idea of using bodies as stash bags has become standard procedure, so they're always looking for fresh packaging materials. Why you tend to feel a little uneasy around Rats: you sense he's always mentally measuring you up, estimating your capacity.

As you ease your abused bod down off the cabinet tray, you can actually hear the ice crystals whisper their little dying snaps and pops, but at least you're defrosted enough to be able to shiver from the cold. You try to remember what happened, but the blow to your head has deleted most of it. Something about a doomed planet. And a doughnut. Or half a doughnut. Makes your head, aching, ache all the worse, trying to think about these things, so you give it up. Your exact words, spoken aloud to all present, are: Fuck it. The Creep is nowhere to be seen, the place deserted. You check your corpus d for scars. There are plenty, but no new ones. You find your clothes dangling from the body hoist above the dissection slab like flayed hides. Still wet. Cold. Tie draped over the hanging organ scale, spotted with chili. Is that a clue? The .22 is still in the jacket pocket, though it has been fired. But the black veil is missing. You wonder if it is hidden somewhere and open the other drawers. In one of them, popping out head forward like a jack-in-the-box, you find the Creep, color: blue, with his nose bandaged from the last time you were here and a bullet hole in his forehead like a beauty spot. Looks like one made by a .22. Not only have you blown your case, you're going to be a wanted man. The Creep's unseeing eyes are wide open, bulging. The ogler still, now ogling death. He once described bonesaw whine as a love song, formaldehyde as an aphrodisiac. You pull his tray all the way out in case the veil is secreted somewhere; it isn't, an unpleasant and futile exercise. His toe tag reads: BIG. Does it refer to the toe it's tied to, or is it a signature? It reminds you to take off your sock and look at your own: THIS LITTLE PIGGY SHOULD STAY HOME.

Your thoughts exactly. How long do you remain loyal to a dead widow who never even lifted her veil for you and from whom there can be no more bankrolls? You pull on the rest of your cold wet togs, tip your fedora down over your nose, turn up your trenchcoat collar, and, before the cops can turn up, head back to

the office under the gray rain, head ringing, your cold
rags sandpapering your skin as you walk. Blanche
meets you at the office door, peering disapprovingly
over her hornrims, and orders you out of your clothes.
This is apparently one of the days she turns up. She
bandages your head, smears lotion on your chafed skin,
remarks on your bleached pubic hair. You hadn't
noticed; proof you can't use that the Creep was shot
after you got filed away. She kneels down to read the
tattoo on what she calls your sit-me-down that says,
she says, in small print, inside a broken heart: YOU ARE
BEING FOLLOWED. You were wondering why it was itching back there. She loans you her silk drawers—you're
getting used to them now, but you're definitely not buying a pair of your own—and takes everything off to the
laundromat. This time it is of course not the widow
who turns up, in peace may she. It's Captain Blue. I've
come to arrest you for murder, Noir, more than one,
but I can't take you in like that. You use bleach? It's dis-
gusting. You'd cause a riot down at the station and lose
those things hanging out before I could even get you
booked. I'll come back in ten minutes, killer. If you
haven't got some goddamned clothes on by then, I'm
going to shoot you.

THAT RAINY MORNING A COUPLE OF WEEKS AGO WHEN the widow found you in Blanche's pink underpants, your bandaged head rocking unsteadily on its stem, all you could think to say was: This is one tough case, lady. Look what they did to me!

What? That? she asked, head tipped toward the undies. Who did?

You looked around for something to wear. All you could find was your hat so you put it on, perching it atop your turban, lit up a cigarette, dangling it sullenly in the corner of your mouth, and sat behind your desk, though sitting hurt. Even worse when, to show that things were cool in spite of appearances, you tried to put your feet up on the desk. Big mistake.

Are you in pain, Mr. Noir?

Just—*ungh!*—worrying about you, kid. You're mixed up with some pretty rough company.

I know that, Mr. Noir. It's why I came to you. What have you found out? Have you been able to follow my husband's business partner?

Working on that. I've been checking into the insurance policy. Seems it might have been invalid if death was by suicide. Would have been important that he died, or seemed to die, by some other means.

I didn't even know he had an insurance policy, she said, worrying her pale fingers in her lap, her multifaceted diamond glinting like coded signals in the dim

light leaking in through the windows, streaming with
rain. Her fragrance was fresh and innocent, yet somehow dangerous. Seductive. When her head dropped a
moment, you made a quick adjustment to your silken
bonds. Better. But not much. Why do some guys like to
wear these things? He never talked about business with
me, she said. She heaved a sigh, her breasts rising and
falling provocatively inside their black lace bodice. I
miss him so.

Though you couldn't see her expression behind
the veil, you could hear the sorrow in her voice. The
fear. Genuine or faked? Who cares? Give the girl a
break. Enjoy yourself. Tell me again how you met your
husband.

I was a poor girl, alone and friendless in the city,
and he was—he advertised for a maid and housekeeper.
He was good enough to hire me, though I had no ref-
erences. I was very grateful.

So to thank him you provided other services . . . ?

What can you possibly mean, Mr. Noir? I of
course did all that was asked of me to the best of my
limited experience. And he was appreciative of my
application and, being of a kind and generous nature,
was always attentive to my needs.

Yeah, sure. But, in a word, how did you get it on?

Get it on? Oh, you mean. . . . How did we fall in
love? You were watching her legs again. She knew you

were watching her legs. She parted them slightly and they seemed almost to release a sigh from within their skirted shadows. There was more of you stretching Blanche's panties now, but oddly you felt less uncomfortable. It happened one day when I was changing out of my work uniform and he passed by. The wind must have blown the door open behind me. I didn't know he was there until I heard him breathing at my back. As he pressed against me I could feel him trembling with emotion, as I was trembling, too. It was all very innocent, but I was at a loss to know what to do. And he was such a handsome man, strong, manly. He could not conceivably have dressed as you are dressed, Mr. Noir.

Too bad, he never knew what he missed. And where was the wife all this time?

I think I told you. The poor woman was bedridden and did not have long to live.

That's how she was when you started undressing there?

Working there? Yes, I think so. Or soon after. The dear man was distraught. He fell to weeping inconsolably on my breast.

While standing, or supine?

Mr. Noir, I do not understand the point of your questions. And would you please put both of your hands on top of the desk where I can watch them?

⊙

IT WAS BLANCHE, LATER, WHO ASKED ALL THE SERIOUS questions. What you asked was: So, what are you doing tonight, sweetheart? We can talk more about all this over supper. But when you looked up, widow wasn't there. She had an interesting way of coming and going. She'd left another roll of bills on the desk, but you had no pockets, so when Blanche returned she picked it up and locked it in her desk drawer. For expenses, she said. We have a lot to do. I have learned that the deceased's estate passes to one of two heirs, but must pass intact, meaning that one of them has to relinquish their share or die. A kind of macabre joke. When you gave her back her undies, she gazed at them with something between repugnance and dismay, then asked you to turn around. What do you know about your client's background, Mr. Noir?

Well, she comes from a small country town with tree-lined streets and green lawns where everybody loves each other.

Sure, she said. And bodies buried under the rose bushes and unspeakable horrors in the family den. I didn't mean that. You can look now. I mean, what do you know about her mother, her brother, her boyfriend, and her father, the drug dealer?

Town pharmacist, you corrected. Your clothes were warm from the dryer and comforting. Still having trouble keeping your brainpod from bobbing about, though, and it was therefore less useful than usual.

Where are they?

You supposed they were back at the farm. What did they have to do with this case?

If her father was supplying her with poison and whatever narcotics her husband was using, then they could all be involved.

But who said—?

And what about the person you're supposed to follow?

I've got a lead on that. Last night. From Snark. That's how I got in trouble.

With Officer Snark?

No. Afterwards. Though he might have been there. The details are blurry. But Snark told me Mister Big has the hots for medieval toy soldiers. I'll buy a few and advertise them and see if I can get a nibble.

The sort of miniatures he would want you can't afford. Not even with the black widow's handouts. You'll have to rent them. I'll look for a dealer.

It is your own comfortable fresh-smelling underwear, warm from the dryer, rags though they be, that
you are looking forward to now. But Blue's ten minutes
are nearly up when Blanche returns empty-handed. The
clothes are still in the dryer, she had to wash them twice
to get the morgue smells out, it will be another twenty
minutes. You can't wait. Blue is due any second. You
turn your back and give Blanche her drawers back (I
hope that tattoo was done with a clean needle, she says
reproachfully), shove your bare feet into your squishy
dogs, pull on your cold wet trenchcoat, drop your .22
and Blanche's skin lotion in the pockets, perch your
fedora atop the bandages, and hurry out, down the
back stairs. At the alley door, you check the mirror
apparatus you've rigged there as a lookout and see that
some lunk is waiting for you outside, cosh in hand.
Blue covering all bets. There's probably somebody on
the fire escape, too. Time for the old straw dummy routine, hoping only this isn't a cop who has already been
burned. You keep the dummy down here, dressed in a
trenchcoat and fedora for just such occasions. Cops.
Landlords. Disappointed clients. Irate husbands. You
spread the dummy head-down on the stairs, unlatch the
door quietly, stand so as to be hidden behind the
opened door, throw an old kitchen chair and cry out:
Oh fuck! Help! Your would-be assailant rushes in and
delivers a blow to the dummy just as you brain him

with the butt of your .22. It's not one of Blue's boys. It's the suit, the Hammer, the thug who accosted you in Loui's Lounge, the one you slugged and were slugged by down at the docks. He's out cold. Your hurting head hurts more to think of how his head will hurt, but just desserts for the dickhead after what he did to you last night. You quickly rifle his jacket pockets, switch your rod with his .45, dart out into the rainy alley. You can hear sirens out front. You take a right, a left, a right, losing yourself in the alleyed labyrinth. Loui's is a good idea. Flame will let you hole up in her room and the food's good.

The alley. You can't say it's your home away from home, having no real home to be away from, but you know it well. You've spent serious time in it. Have been mugged, chased, blown, asked for a light, beaten up, paid off, conned, dumped, supplied, scared shitless, given hot tips, shortchanged, shot at in here. You say, here. The alley is not on any streetmap. It is under it somewhere. Or behind it. It is negotiated intuitively; maps are useless, maybe even deceptive. Even in the rain, its scabrous brick walls are layered with shadows, worn like old rags. It is not uninhabited. It has its pimps and dealers, street tramps, smalltime grifters, misnamed homeless (they know where their home is better than you do), muggers, psychopaths, deviants. Not unlike City Hall, in short, or any church or company boardroom. You have to keep your eye out for one of them in particular. Known as Mad Meg, she likes to leap out of the shadows and stab people with her rusty kitchen knife. Once an honest stripper, but misused by a sadistic sugar daddy who pumped her full of brain-burning opiates, thrown out on the streets when her mind went and her body bagged, now the hidden princess of the alley. Like the alley, she's treacherously complex yet rough on the surface and without façade, oddly innocent or at least neutrally unmotivated even as she lunges at her victims, somewhat pestilential, smelling of urine and half-blind, the indecorous back-side of the human condition, the poxy dead end we all try to avoid. She's a friend of yours though she doesn't always remember that. You bring her things that she collects like coat buttons, swizzle sticks, shoelaces, candy wrappers, and old tennis balls, and once she got you out of a scrape by attacking the killer who was attacking you, though that may have just been the luck of who was on top. You have nothing to give her today except Blanche's lotion or your own laces, but no need, she remains hidden.

Not that your route to Loui's is without incident. You witness a murder for one thing. You've just stepped into an abandoned bicycle shed to get out of the downpour when you see two figures at the other end of the alley dragging a third, mere shadowy outlines as though the rain were a drawn blind between you with dim silhouettes playing on it. Through the rain's rattle you can hear one of them giving orders, the other whining in reply in a squeaky voice. The guy giving the orders does not sound like a street mug. He turns to go, but Squeaky returns and pumps a round of bullets into the victim's head. Psycho. The boss scolds him in a father-to-son way and leads him off. Sirens sound. Can't stay. Who was it? Never know. One of life's little mysteries.

ONE WET DAY'S END YOU WERE TAILING A GUY THROUGH here who you thought might be Mister Big. This was after you'd delivered your illustrated classified ad for the toy soldiers to the city newsrag. Through a friendly dealer, Blanche had learned of a private collector who owned a unique set of figures from the Battle of Agincourt with brigandines made out of mouse leather and bascinets of silver with hinged visors, stuffed and quilted gambesons on the French crossbowmen, knee-length hauberks of silver chain mail on the English archers, beards and horse tails of real hair with brass and leather trappings for the horses, honed steel swords, velvet surcoats, and silken jupons (see what you learn in this racket), and she was able to get permission to photograph some of the figures for a philosophical journal she claimed to edit, though insurance for the day cost half the widow's roll. The ad promised a private showing to genuine collectors only, and the newspapers had not even hit the streets before the calls started coming in.

You left Blanche to fend off the queries, waiting for the one phone call that mattered, and went out for a beer. Several actually, ending up at Loui's talking with Joe the bartender about the meaning of life, having by now switched to the hard stuff. Joe's view in sum was that life was full of sickness, loneliness, corruption, cruelty, paranoia, betrayal, murder, cynicism, impotence, and fear, and then there was the dark side. Sometimes you gotta just dummy up and let your pants fall where they may, he said, somewhat enigmatically. You realized that what was wrong with Joe was that he was a teetotaler.

Across the room at a dining table sat a fat guy in a white linen suit with a napkin tucked into his shirt collar, delicately putting away the back half of a cow. Rings on all his fingers, even his thumbs. He looked familiar. Joe didn't know who he was but said he was a loner who came in from time to time to eat a few dinners. Probably you'd seen him in here before. Joe thought he might be a thin guy disguised as a fat guy.

Maybe. But he sure eats like a fat guy. Everything but the tail and horns.

He sometimes has those with cheese and coffee, Joe said.

On a hunch (a hunch is to a gumshoe what a skirt is to a letch: a tease; pursuit; trouble), when he lit up a cigar, paid, donned his panama, and left, you decided to step out into the drizzle and follow him. You knew zip plus toy soldiers about Mister Big, but you figured it was likely his nickname was for more than power alone. Even if the guy was only a mock-Mister B, it might be interesting to see where he goes, and you'd have something to report to the widow the next time she turned up. At first you were on the street, watching in the classic surveillance manner his slow waddling movements in the reflections of shop windows, but then at some point you were in the alley. How that happens is almost always a mystery. You have privileged access to it down your back stairs, maybe everyone does, but if you step out the front door the alley is hard to find. You can't see it and then, what do you know, you're in it. The fat man in the panama and linen suit zigzagged along, never looking back, but you had the feeling he knew you were back there, paddling through the garbage, trying to pretend you were just out for your daily constitutional. It was probably time to forget it and turn around, but you weren't sure where you were and were as likely to find your way out going forwards as backwards. And, besides, the more you followed him, the more convinced you were that this was the guy you were looking for. He was moving faster and faster, he maybe ate like a fat man but he moved like a thin man, maybe Joe was right, it was hard to keep up. Finally, he was running flat out, pivoting sharply around corners like a mechanical carnival target on ball bearings, hopping nimbly over obstacles, darting down narrow passageways, somehow skirting puddles that you splashed through, a pale luminosity flitting through the moist shadowy alley like a will-o'-the-wisp, and soon you were only catching fleeting glimpses of him in the distance and then you lost him altogether.

You leaned against a boarded-up door to get your breath, torch a fag. Where were you? No idea. But you could hear rustlings, knew you'd been had, knew your situation was dangerous. You'd pocketed what remained of the widow's roll for operating expenses (Blanche on the phone rolled her eyes and shook her yellow curls) and though you'd blown some of it in Loui's there was plenty left and you worried now about getting mugged, or worse. These guys could smell money like sniffer dogs, even in the rain, and they usually preferred to ice their victims rather than merely threaten them, as it gave them more undisturbed pocket-poking time. The alley branched out in five or six directions from here, mostly you supposed into rat-infested dead ends where killers lurked. Your .22 was back in the office; you had nothing to defend yourself with except your fists. Glancing around for a weapon of some sort, your eye fell on a big ivory coat button and, keeping your back to the wet wall, you snatched it up in case you ran into Mad Meg. Beyond it was an old yellow tennis ball soaking in a puddle, and beyond that a red plastic swizzle stick. The swizzle stick was in front of what looked at first glance like a back door, but turned out to be a low underpass into another dark tangle of alleyways. A brass button off a military coat, a knotted shoelace, another bald tennis ball, a green-and-gold candy wrapper. These objects might have fallen out of Meg's bagged household effects as she passed through here, or she might have dropped them on purpose. Either way, following their trail was your only shot. At the very least, if you came upon her, you could maybe wrestle the kitchen knife away from her, use it to fight your way out of here. It was a kind of scavenger hunt, chased by muffled footsteps, tumbling ashcan lids, the squawk of a startled cat being kicked.

Suddenly, picking up a pair of crimson-and-blue ice-skate shoelaces, you found yourself in a blind alley. A trap? An aluminum candy wrapper lay like a lottery ticket in front of a puckery patch of wet asphalt. There was a day-glo orange tennis ball, bright as fresh fruit, beyond the patch in front of the windowless brick wall that closed off the alley, but on your left, closer by, between two battered ashcans standing like woebegone sentries, lay a swizzle stick with a little flag on it that you remembered giving her. Mad Meg had saluted it, then picked her nose with it. You chose that over the orange ball, and as you stooped to pick it up, a red-eyed assailant in old army fatigues came charging out of a shadowy hole in the opposite wall with a switchblade. Oh shit. You braced yourself, yanking one of the ashcans in front of yourself, but when the guy stepped onto the puckery patch, that was as far as he got: his feet stuck, sank, the asphalt sucking him down, his screams smothered by the falling rain. There was a final wet sucking sound and your attacker was gone, nothing left but the switchblade and the echo of his final curse. You skirted the patch to gather up the orange tennis ball, saw the pink cloth-coat button in the mouth of the hole in the wall whence your attacker came, crouched down, picked it up, and crept through.

You were in the alleyway behind your office building. You left your collection of memorabilia in the hole along with a button ripped from your own trench-coat and the switchblade. All right, it made Meg all the more dangerous next time she rushed you, but you owed her as much.

The office was dark. Blanche had left. There was a full-page note detailing all the incoming calls. Three had seemed promising enough to send them photographs (they were marked). She also left her panties. In case you need these, her note said. That Blanche.

You were exhausted from your ordeal in the alley and went over to lie down on the sofa, but somebody was already lying there. A dead body? No. Your client, the widow. Still veiled and primly sheathed in black, but her shoes were off. There's something more I should tell you, Mr. Noir, she said.

⊙

AT LOUI'S, HAVING MADE IT THROUGH THE SODDEN alley dressed only in your trench and spongy gums, you explain you're on the lam from the law and have to lay low for a time. But Loui has a problem with that, Flame, too. It turns out Blue has already been here, asking questions, making threats of arrest and worse. The place might get closed down, Loui says, and there's a cop on the force Flame refused to play kinky games with who might be looking to get back at her.

It's a bum rap, Loui. Somebody shot the morgue attendant with my gun while I was out cold and on ice in the crypt.

Loui, his bald pate sweating, is sympathetic, but

no dice. There are others, too, the bodies are piling up. He is chewing his manicured nails and casting nervous glances over his shoulder and, much as he loves you, he wants you to move on. Flame says: The buckwheat in the suit has been here, too, asking for you. Blondie, she adds admiringly, helping you out of your soggy trench-coat.

Yeah, the Hammer. I met him on the way.

Loui is insistent in his wheedling way, but Flame takes pity on your cold wet naked condition (Joe the bartender clucks disparagingly at the sight, pours you a brandy) and offers you her changing room for the night, provided you stay hidden in the wardrobe cupboard if she has any company. I can take care of the captain in ways Loui can't, she says. Loui, scowling, disappears into his office with a bottle. Just have to hope he doesn't turn stoolie and call Blue in. Flame and Joe read your toe tag and agree that it's good advice but know you'll never follow it, stubborn dickhead that you are.

In the changing room, Flame applies a soothing ointment to the festering tattoo (it has been itching and you've been scratching at it with dirty fingernails), works Blanche's lotion into your chafed hide, and warms other parts with her tongue, bemusedly combing your bleached hair with her long red nails. Your other hair is still wrapped in bandages. She wants to know who it is that's following you. You don't know. Haven't even noticed. She offers you a frilly bathrobe and a pair of Victorian bloomers from her days as a stag-film actress. They are more comfortable than Blanche's, but open in the crotch so they don't hold anything. She says she'll get word to Blanche that you're here so she can drop your clothes by before you head off tomorrow and tells you to lie down on the chaise lounge and she'll tell you a story.

WHEN I WAS JUST A KID, PHIL, THIS GUY TOOK ME under his wing. I knew he was trouble, he had badboy written all over him—literally, around each nipple and his navel like eye sockets and down the length of his dick, though when it was hard, it said: BEARDED BALONEY — but I was young and madly in love, and brutal as he was to others, he treated me like a princess. Of course, he was insanely jealous. I didn't dare look at another man—it was like a death sentence. Any guy who looked my way and grinned or winked or called out something simply disappeared. Sometimes I thought I could use this as a kind of magic power to erase people I had a grudge against, like the guy who first raped me, for example. But I don't hold grudges long and in truth, after the rough stuff was over, that guy and I became friends and sometime lovers and I wished him no harm. Just the same, he made an attempt to get hold of me, thinking I might be in trouble, and that was the end of him. Badboy had a little gun that went "spat!" when you fired it. That's all, just "spat!" and some guy's motor didn't work any more. He had a twin brother who was a cop and they loved and hated each other the way brothers do, and several times had tried to kill each other, but maybe without enough conviction. Badboy ran a bigtime protection and extortion racket, and the crooked chief of police was one of many under his thumb. The chief wanted him dead and out of his life, and assigned Badboy's cop brother to nailing him for his crimes, telling him to bring him in dead or alive, knowing which way it would have to be. My lover knew all this from friends on the force. He also heard that his brother had his eye on me or wanted him to think he did. One of the two—I'm not sure which, their voices were just alike, but probably the cop brother—called me and told me what your tattoo is telling you. Well, this was scary. I realized I was being used, without being able to do anything about it, to set a trap. And if it was my lover who had called me, it was even worse, especially when I discovered his little spat-gun in my purse. Or one just like it. Was I supposed to kill the guy following me? The cop, one would think, but my lover often followed me out of jealousy. I felt like a character in two different stories at the same time, as if the twin brothers had doubled me, too. I was setting the trap in one life, springing it in the other, and helpless in both. I didn't know what to do, but then . . .

IT'S A GOOD STORY AND YOU WANT TO KNOW MORE (gotta know, gotta know), but you can't help it, you fall asleep, and from there the story takes other turnings of its own. You become her lover, or else the cop, and the other guy is the fat man in the white suit and panama hat you once tailed through the alley. Are you his double? No, this is a different caper. Nevertheless, you are quite fat and you cannot move very fast. You also have the disadvantage of being dressed in women's underwear. Maybe you are the Flame person, not the lover or the cop. The widow is in it, but more like the chief of police. *Her* brother is in it somewhere and he is said also to be wearing women's underpants and a bra. You both have toe tags. Is he your double? No, you don't have a bra. Things are becoming clear at last, the case is almost solved. At the same time, you are about to be shot. Neither happens. You wake up.

I think Joe put something in my drink to knock me out, you say.

Yeah. It's called alcohol. It's morning, handsome, and your clothes are here. We had another visit from Blue and his boys last night. Time to hit the road, Phil. You're not safe in this place.

When does a man get a breakfast in this life? you want to know, but the question is received as a gratuitous comment. You return Flame's bloomers and pull on your own clothes, laundered, pressed, and folded: the old black pinstripe suit with the baggy knees and threadbare elbows, a white shirt, frayed but clean and crisply starched, dark tie, and black socks and shoes, holes in the heels of the former, in the soles of the other. Blanche has already folded a white handkerchief into the jacket lapel pocket, dropped a loaded bill clip in the pants. Collar and tie pins, cuff links, rumpled fedora, borrowed .45 in your trenchcoat pocket. In short, a somewhat seedy version of any self-respecting gangster's threads.

There's a basement link to the bookies next door, they'll show you the safe route from there, Flame says, handing you sandwiches and a bottle in a brown paper bag and a passkey and slapping your butt affectionately. See you, baby.

WHEN YOUR LATE DEPARTED CLIENT, THE VEILED widow, turned up on your couch in your darkened office after your mazy trials in the alley, she also had a story about a brother. My brother has come to the city, she said from under her veil, peaked by the tip of her nose. He says he has come to protect me, but he is a naïve boy, easily influenced, and I fear for him here. And for myself.

The football player.

No, basketball. Does that make a difference?

His hands.

Oh, I see. His hands?

Listen, I'm bushed, kid. Mind if I stretch out there beside you while you tell me your story?

I certainly do mind, Mr. Noir. You stay where you are. My brother, as I have suggested, is a likeable easygoing fellow, a playful smalltown boy with a big heart who, in spite of our father's stern discipline, is inclined to get into ridiculous trouble from time to time. Often this is due to his rather singular passion for hardboiled detective novels and films. He is an impressionable fellow and he likes to act out what he has seen or read, or perhaps he feels compelled to, driven by some inner need to create a persona for himself, otherwise lacking.

Well, there are worse lives to take up than a private eye's, you grumbled, somewhat defensively. Her hands, not those of a basketball player, were folded softly on her belly. Not much flesh was visible; you had to enjoy what there was. They were crowned, as a small knoll might be crowned by a lighthouse, by her large glittering ring. A lure. For catching bigger fish than you.

I am afraid, Mr. Noir, that it excites him rather to emulate the villains. She sighed and her hands rose and fell as if lifted by a gentle wave. So he has robbed some banks, turned to gambling and easy women, killed a few people, and so on, behavior that may well be tolerated in the city, but is not acceptable in our little town. He submits meekly to our father's chastisements after each episode, but seems drawn ineluctably toward a life of flamboyant crime. The romance novels I have bought him appear to have had no effect at all.

She was flexing her toes in her black stockings as a bird of prey might. You wondered if she painted her toenails. Her toe-flexing caused her thighs to ripple faintly under the black skirt. If she lifts one knee, you thought, she's going to have to fight you off. So, you and your brother are not getting on, and you think—

Oh no, on the contrary. We love each other very much—too much, some say, reflecting the oppressive misunderstandings that prevail in small communities such as ours—but that's just the point. Just think, Mr. Noir. To be the perfect villain, one would have to try to kill that which he most loves, and it would be all the more villainous to accept money from others for doing so.

Others? A rhetorical question. You knew the plot here, at least as devised or imagined by the widow. What you really wanted to know was what she and her brother were up to to set off those oppressive misunderstandings.

I have reason to believe he has taken employment with that man whose name I have given you. The one you are supposed to be following. Have you any news?

Well, I had an eye on him just now, or someone like him, but he got away.

You must be more assiduous, she said, and that wave rolled under her hands once more. I am depending on you, Mr. Noir. My life is in your hands. She turned her head to look at them, the veil flattening over her cheek and dropping off her nose, and you looked at them: gnarled, calloused, muddied by the alley muck you'd been crawling through, the fingernails filthy, the knuckles made knobby by frequent breakage. You opened them up and stared into their palms. They looked like death to you. Maybe to her, too. She was no longer looking at them, her beak poking up at the ceilinged shadows as before. It was as if she had given up on them. In one of your most celebrated cases, all you had to work with was a severed hand. From the part you were able to deduce the whole and, indirectly, solve a crime. You were younger then and drinking less. You have implied that my father may have behaved improperly with me, she said at last, and, alas, that is true. My dear sweet mother had stopped baking pies and had slipped into some crippling addiction and spent the day cursing the deity. I had no one else to turn to, so I asked my brother to hide in the closet the next time my father visited and, if necessary, to come to my rescue. But instead, he only kept watching. After that, he was always in the closet. I thought that letting him do what father did would end this perverse behavior, but it was not the sight of me that excited him. It was father.

Outside the window, the buzzing neon light blinked eerily. Wheeling police car lights flickered on the ceiling like some kind of primitive motion picture machine showing a film whose images time had dissolved. You were trying to see there what the brother saw. And the lover? you asked. What happened to him? In the darkness, her hands had faded away. You felt like you were talking to a dark shadow on the dark couch. Hello? You *were* talking to a shadow. There being no objection, you lay down with it.

SLEEPING WITH SHADOWS. IF LIFE IS AT BEST A SHADOW play, with what or whom else do we ever sleep, in spite of the fleshy illusions of the moment? Such was the principal burden of the Case of the Severed Hand. The hand was waiting outside your office door one morning as if it had strolled there on its fingertips. Had it been left there as a warning? An appeal for help? Did you know its former owner? Severed body parts are commonplace in the workaday life of a private dick. You picked it up and carried it into your office and tossed it in the in-box.

At the time you were on well-paid assignment from a humorless crook-backed old hock shop owner and fence for stolen goods named Crabbe. According to his story, some goods belonging to a murder victim had passed through his hands and he was being black-mailed by a bent cop who threatened to hang the murder on him if he didn't pay up. I'm just a businessman, he growled. I have no idea what fucking murder he's talking about, one forgettable rich bastard or another, but I know my situation ain't good. Crabbe figured the cop was working for the mayor, known for his shake-down rackets, so he couldn't go to the guy's superiors. He knew you as one who took no shit from city hall and bore the scars to prove it and believed he could count on you. As Blanche, cleaning your office, liked to say: Your horror of gratuities from officialdom, Mr.

Noir, is matched only by your horror of cleanliness. The cop was on his tail and your job was to tail the tail and log his movements. Presumably so Crabbe could steer clear of him and look for ways to put the black-mailer on the defensive.

You had spotted the guy, followed him for awhile. Big thuggish lout with a chain-smoking habit, a pocket flask from which he sucked freely, and a dark scowl. Mean-looking slow-moving sonuvabitch, well armed. But why would a blackmailer tail his victim, you won-dered. The usual drill is to set payoff schedules and oth-erwise keep out of sight. You had to see Rats on a shop-ping trip, so you described the cop and Rats said he knew him, bruiser named Snark. Weird fuck but straight. Which meant that the old pawnbroker, run-ning from the law, probably had a hit man ready to strike when you gave him the pattern of the cop's movements.

So what now? Turn on your employer and squeal to the cops? Give Crabbe back his money (which you'd already spent) and drop out, letting the bodies fall where they may? Send in false data and risk getting taken out yourself? But weren't you running that risk anyway? You were asking these questions out loud. You realized you'd been interrogating, not your glass of whiskey as is your habit, but the hand in your in-box. You took it out and set it on your desk on its thumb and rigid fingers like a pentapod and, taking a long slug, asked: And what about you, sweetheart? Where'd you come from? A woman's hand, you felt certain. When, some time later, you first saw the widow's hands in her lap you were somewhat reminded of it, but the severed hand had longer fingers, bonier knuckles, stubby fingertips like those of a professional pianist, a thin but sinewy wrist; it was well-tanned and bore three small rings, none of them a match for the widow's rock. Curious, though: a lapis lazuli winged scarab with hieroglyphs, intertwined gold and white gold serpents with ruby eyes, and a carved bloodstone ring with some sort of Arabic inscription. So something of an exotic dame, a dancer maybe. Acrobat. Fortune teller. The long expressive fingers, hard unpainted nails, sharp knuckles suggested to you that she had long healthy bones, was tall, erect, lithe. Your type. One of them.

Thus, you assembled her from what the hand told you. It began as a lark, but became increasingly obsessive. You turned the hand over, examined the pads on her thumb and fingers, the flesh on her palm: Small breasts, you thought. Slender hips. You checked out her life and luck lines, what her palm said about her heart and head, her fate. You were no adept, they said nothing. That she'd had a misfortunate life you didn't need her palm to tell you, the raw wound at the wrist said it

all. By the fine hairs on the back of the hand, you figured she was auburn-haired. With brown eyes? Because
of the bloodstone maybe, you guessed green. You saw
a tall slender auburn-haired green-eyed beauty with a
stub where the right hand should be. Wearing? The
sequined briefs and halter of a circus aerialist maybe.
Or gypsy silks. For the moment, nothing at all. Though
she stood at some distance from you, an expression of
ineffable longing (for you? for her hand?) on her high-
boned face, she seemed at the same time to be explor-
ing your body, opening up your trousers, crawling into
them, and you realized that the hand was operating on
its own. Or perhaps still belonged to her in some manner. Her other hand was between her thighs. Which
were exquisitely beautiful. You ached to hold her and,
by reaching out, though you couldn't see your hands,
that seemed possible, and as you wrapped your mitts
around her amazing hams she began to quiver and
twist, her jaw dropping open, her green eyes glazing
over. And while you were holding her in that strange
way, fascinated by her snaky writhings, the hand began
crawling up your body toward your face. You tried to
reach for it to push it away, but your hands were past-
ed to her behind. You understood immediately as it
gripped your cheek bones and reached inside your
mouth that it intended to screw off your head and you
awoke in a sweat on your leather sofa, the hand resting

on your face. You must have fallen asleep while studying it. Your pants were a mess. More work for poor
Blanche.

Thereafter, she began to dampen your dreams
incessantly with her erotic haunting and, with the help
of Rats' pharmaceuticals (the hand had succeeded),
you slept as often as you could. A femme fatale, yes,
but of an eerie sort. You showed the hand to a counterfeiter you knew, a pal of Rats, explaining that you
were on a murder case, the hand your only clue, and
asked him to do a sketch based on your description of
what you called your scientific reconstruction of the
whole from the part, a sketch you hung on the wall
over your desk like the portrait of a president. Without
pants. Something to stare at during those brief inter-
ludes between sleep. You'd lost interest in the Crabbe
case, having gone the false data route, stalling for time,
and might have forgotten about the snarling old pawnbroker entirely had he not shown up one rainy afternoon in your office, awakening you from a dream in
which you were at sea, afloat in the cup of the
upturned hand, tethered by your unseen hands to the
hips of the green-eyed beauty swaying on the shore
while the winged scarab fluttered in your crotch.
Crabbe glanced up at the counterfeiter's drawing, then
at the hand perched on your desktop, turned white.
How did you get this? he gasped. He grabbed up the

hand, drew a gun, pointed it at your head. Which was when you met Snark. He called out from the doorway and when Crabbe spun to fire, you had a mortally wounded pawnbroker on your office floor with just enough life left in him for Snark to extract a full confession. It turned out Snark had been pursuing Crabbe for murder. No, he said, the body had both hands and looked nothing like the drawing, being more of the dippy overfed bleach-blond heiress sort, but Crabbe was probably feeling guilty and saw his victim everywhere. And why don't you button up there, that's a truly ugly sight. It wasn't the hand that startled the pawnbroker, Snark went on to explain, picking up your phone to call in the meat wagon, but the rings, which had belonged to the victim and had been peddled by Crabbe to an undercover cop. Snark's contortionist wife used an ancient mummified hand in a trick in which she seemed to swallow her arm, the hand appearing from an aperture lower down, though the highest part of her during the act. Fooled me the first time, Snark said and took a deep drink from the neck of your whiskey bottle. I was afraid to put my thing in there again for fear of the hand grabbing it and not letting go, until she showed me how the trick worked. He'd figured that mounting the stolen rings on the mummy's hand and leaving it somewhere Crabbe was sure to see it might freak the murderer out and elicit an admission of guilt, as it did.

Yeah, but if you hadn't turned up when you did, pal, I'd be fucking fly bait.

So what? We'd have caught him just the same and would've had two murders to pin on him instead of one.

Snark picked up the hand and stuffed it in a pocket. You were sorry to see it go. I was hoping to keep it around as a back scratcher, you said. By the way, what does that Arabic inscription on the ring say?

It's Persian. Guy who read it for me said it was a racing tip. Something like put ten on number three in the fifth.

WHICH, PASSING THROUGH THE BOOKIES' BASEMENT, taking the smugglers' route to the docks, is what you do now, just as you've done every week for years now. Ten on number three in the fifth. Yet another futile romantic gesture. Your one-handed green-eyed love withdrew from your dreams when Snark took the severed hand away, although once, a year or so later, you found yourself in a horse race with the hand as your tottering mount, your dick ringed with the intertwined serpents and urging the hand on, she waiting in vain for you at the distant finish line, too far away even for disembodied dream hands to reach. What did that dream mean? You never ask.

The smugglers' route is a series of interlinked cellars, some with nothing but a locked door between them, opened with the passkey Flame gave you, others requiring a crawl on your pinstripes through dark damp tunnels. You travel mostly by night, curling up behind furnaces by day, snaking your way to the docklands. What are you going to do when you get there? Can't stay underground forever. Somehow you have to find out who really killed the Creep. Why Fingers bought it. Whose was the heap that ran him down. What Rats was trying to tell you. You decide to check in with your man Snark, get the latest rumble. Which means going topside to find a phone booth, risk getting caught. Chance you have to take. You're in an expansive basement broken up into a warren of changing and makeup rooms. Theater of some kind. Pinned-up pix suggest a burlesque house. You don't recognize the dancers, but it has been awhile. There's a back stairs to the stage door, but no phone booth outside. Just a wet dirty side street, lit only by the red light over the door. You have better luck at the corner: phone box under a streetlamp about a block away. Misty streets eerily deserted. Your tattoo is itching, reminding you someone's on your ass, and you sense him there as though he'd been waiting here for you to bubble up out of the concrete. If it's one of Blue's cops, why doesn't he just nab you? Ergo, it's not one of Blue's cops. Some guy who works for Mister Big? The gorilla who tried to kill you down at the docks, then accosted you behind your office?

It's after midnight, Snark is not happy you've called. Ring me back some other fucking time, Noir. I'm eating a pretzel, as you might say.

Sorry, can't do that, Snark. I'm on the run and being followed. I just want you to know I didn't kill that guy.

Which guy are you talking about?

The morgue attendant. There's more than one?

Some beef in a suit seen hanging around outside the alley door of your office building has been found shot dead in another part of the alley.

The Hammer? The guy who tried to kill me down at pier four. I think I saw him get taken out. Two guys. One with a squeaky voice.

He'd been shot in the head several times with your .22.

That's because I'd kayoed the poor sonuvabitch on my back stairs and switched rods. I'm packing his .45.

Well. Blue might buy that, might not.

⊙

SO IT CAN'T BE THE HAMMER WHO'S TAILING YOU.
Maybe Fat Agnes? When you told Blanche the next day
about chasing the fat man in the white suit who turned
into a kind of will-o'-the-wisp and led you into a mazy
death trap, she said: Ignis fatuus. What? Will-o'-the-
wisp. Ignis fatuus. Like those black seams you used to
chase. Thus, Fat Agnes. You realized you'd glimpsed
him often. In Loui's, outside your office on the street
below, standing on a bridge overlooking the docklands,
at the Chinese buffet (closed down shortly after), in line
at the post office, at the fights. Someone you spotted
out of the corner of your eye when distracted with
something or someone else, but who wasn't there when
you were able to turn and look, nothing left but maybe
a trace of his sweet cigar smoke. Was it just a coincidence he was so often somewhere in the picture? You
didn't think so. Blanche went on running the toy soldiers ad, tabulating the inquiries, sending out photos to
some, waiting for the call from Mister Big, and one day
Blanche gave you a thumbs-up signal and handed you
the phone. Some guy named Marle who said he represented a bigtime buyer and wanted you to meet him in
the Vendome Café, bring along a few of the figures.
You said you'd bring photos. There was a hesitation

before he agreed. Was he muttering to someone? You decided to go armed.

The Vendome Café was a dimly lit joint near the arena where the scalpers hung out, offering straight sales or a poker game at the back with tickets as their stakes. As soon as you stepped into the place, you smelled the cigar. And there he was, poised serenely at a back table in his white three-piece suit and fob watch chain, his panama on the table alongside a teacup like a signboard. Fat Agnes. As you drew near, you were struck by the way his little cleft chin sat like a bauble in the middle of his neck folds. No jaw line. Sad blue eyes. Button nose. A few strands of colorless hair combed across the top of his dome. He looked startled as you approached him as if about to grab up his panama and run. Hey, mister, are you Noir? some guy asked at the table you'd just passed. It was Marle. You were mistaken. When you looked back, Fat Agnes was gone. Just a cigar butt in an ashtray, still smoldering.

Marle affected a goatee and granny glasses, a leather jacket, black string tie. You showed him the photos with your left hand, ready to draw with your right. He glanced at them cursorily, said he'd have to see the miniatures themselves. You said you'd show them only to the buyer he represented. There were four other leather-jacketed guys at different tables all watching you. You figured they were together. You also figured you were zoning in on your target. You nodded at them all and left. It was the closest you ever got to Fat Agnes, but you heard from Marle again.

⊙

BEFORE YOU HANG UP (YOU SKIP THE BREAK-IN, YOUR visit to the Shed) you book a bill-dipping meet with Snark at the Star Diner, hoping you can make it, there are a lot of things you've got to talk about, then you hurry back through the misty night to the burlesque house. But there's no red light, no stage door. You must have taken a wrong turning. You double back to get your bearings, cannot find the phone booth. Probably you've been winding your way through the smugglers' burrows too long, you're disoriented. You spy just a brief flicker of white at the far end of the street like a butterfly wing. Then darkness again. You know that a shot could ring out in the night, the last thing you'd hear. You press up against the wall of a building, eyes alert in all directions, and sidle along warily, sniffing the wet night air. You might be able to find the docklands by nose alone.

You reach a corner and, drawing the .45, throw yourself around it, crashing into a young girl in fancy but disheveled duds staggering your way on the lonely street. If the collision hadn't knocked the gun out of your hand, you might have shot her. A kid still in her teens. She has been drinking but that's probably the least of it. She stands there, weaving confusedly, trying to focus on you, a stray black curl swaying prettily on her forehead, then she falls into your arms. Take me home? she pleads wispily.

A lone cab rolls by out of the night and you hail it. The address she gives the cabbie is in a spiffy part of town. In the cab, she collapses against your shoulder and drops off, her childish hand falling, as if by accident, between your legs. Knowing winks and grimaces from the pug-faced cabbie in the rearview mirror. You wonder if you've seen him somewhere before. The dozing kid, snoring softly, nuzzles in under your chin, her hand absently stroking your crotch as it might a cat. You take it away from there, wrap it around your waist and she moans in her sleep. Wayward offspring of the decadent rich, you've known her type, been burned before.

When you arrive, she mutters drowsily: My purse? All her sentences are questions. The purse is full of loose money, big bills, too big to hand the cabbie. You pay him double out of your own pocket, but he still calls you a cheap bastard (or maybe a cheating bastard, you're not sure; true, you've pocketed one of the big bills in exchange, he's seen that), raising a finger at you. You try to grab it to break it, but he's gone and you're left clutching at night air. Then silence. This part of town is dead still.

The girl is unable to walk, you're going to have to carry her up to the house. Which is one of those glitzy four-story suburban mansions with turrets and balconies sitting on an acre of sloping manicured lawn. It's a long hike up to the front door with a hundred pounds in your arms and you're pooped when you reach it, though you've been entertained by the pretty sight as her skirt fell away when you picked her up. Little bunny rabbits down there. It's your intention to dump her and drift off into the night, but she's completely out. You lay her on an ornamental bench, search her purse for the house key, accept another bill for expenses. Carrying charges. No key. The door's locked. May have to break in through a window. Which are mostly barred at ground level and of the leaded-glass sort. It's a shot in the dark, but you try your smugglers' route passkey. It works.

You carry the kid inside, looking for a place to set her down, and she comes around long enough to say: Second floor? Thus, with questions, she guides you up the circular balustrade and down the chandeliered hall to her bedroom, which is itself bigger than most houses you've been in, with winking starlights on the ceiling, her bed the size of your efficiency flop.

You drop her on it and she says: Jammies? Second drawer?

I've got you this far, sweetheart. You're on your own.

Please . . . ?

⊙

WHEN YOU FIRST SET OUT YOUR SHINGLE, YOU IMAG-ined being involved in exotic complicated crimes, having to solve them with your wits, do the hero act when things got rough, walk away from the praise after, lighting up a smoke, but in fact you were mostly hired to tail adulterous spouses and get the goods on them. You knew less about sex than you knew about sleuthing, but you soon figured out what the goods were and got them. You were not so much a private eye as an eyer of privates. Your university days. You were good at it, but even so, your clients looked down their noses at you. You were a kid and they had grown-up problems, thought they did. So you were naturally flattered to meet someone who wanted your services and looked up to you, an affectionate little sex kitten a few years your junior, ignorant of the private detective racket and willing to pay whatever you asked. And a more interesting case, too: a missing person. Her sister.

She was afraid of her parents, believing they
might have had something to do with her sister's disappearance and worried something like it might
happen to her, but they were off traveling somewhere, so she was able to take you home with her to
show you some photos, her sister's diary, a glove of
which the mate was missing, her sister's perfume, her
underwear, anything that might help you locate the
missing girl. She told you, rather breathlessly, everything she could remember about her sister, and
especially the days just before she disappeared, and,
taking your hand, gazing up at you adoringly, led you
room by room through the family manor according
to the thread of her story. Which had to do with a
row her sister supposedly had just before her parents
left on their previously unannounced travels. Vague
threats. You weren't sure if the story she was telling
you held together, but solving the case was no longer
foremost on your mind. You just liked to hear her
talk and to feel her innocent little body rubbing up
against yours. Also innocent. Was the missing sister
alive or dead, and, if dead, who killed her and why?
You didn't really care. Maybe her sister was not
really missing and this was just a ruse to lure you
here to get laid. This was the theory you favored. So
when she proposed a cooling-off late-night dip in the
pool, you tucked your pencil behind your ear and

flashing the insouciant smile you'd been practicing in front of your mirror, said, Sure, kid, why not?

She led you out to the pool and took off her clothes and, since you were a tad slow off the mark, helped you out of yours. Did you consider the possibility that, if the sister was dead and the parents got sent to the chair for murder or failed to survive their travels, she'd inherit the family fortune? Maybe in the back of your mind, you did, but women's pubic hair was still fairly new to you and most of your attention was focused on that. That and the slightly embarrassing evidence of your throbbing excitement. She took hold of it as she might a pump handle, triggering instant convulsions, and then, with a mischievous grin, gave it and you, laughing giddily, a push into the pool. She's great! you were thinking as you went under. This is fun! But then you glimpsed something at the bottom of the pool that shouldn't be there: a naked girl's body. You dove down to it, worked the weights off the neck and ankles, and, gasping for breath, hauled her, still soft and warm, to the surface. Which was when you met Blue, then just a rookie cop in homicide, eager to show his stuff and win his merit badges. He was standing at the edge of the pool along with another eight to ten of his grinning pals with automatic rifles aimed at your head, the sex kitten in her pajamas and bathrobe weeping somewhere in the background.

You'd been in some rough street fights, but you hadn't taken a real beating before then. Blue was nothing if not thorough. There was little of you left ignored. Coshes, fists, nightsticks, rubber hose, boots. Some of it while blindfolded, some not. Your further education. Principles of Getting Fucked Over 101. Through it all you stuck by your story because it was the only story you had. C'mon, Noir, he barked, slapping you up one side of the head, then slapping you up the other. We caught you stark naked hugging the corpus delicti. You're a fucking necrophiliac. What more is there to know? That I'm a private detective, that I got hired by that kid to find her missing sister, that she was the one who pushed me into the pool, and that when I saw the dead girl I dove down and brought her up. I figure the kid killed her and needed a fallguy. You're a goddamned liar, Noir. You're gonna get the chair for this. Lie detector tests were the thing in those days. You passed with flying colors. But then so did the sex kitten. Blue never believed you, has never been able to forgive you for spoiling his first big case, still thinks of you as a pervert and a killer and maybe worse if there is worse.

So you should know better. You *do* know better. Just the same (this kitten's soft pleading voice, sweet milky aroma, her damp bunnies—what can you do?), you pull off her shoes and socks, her skirt, go get the pajamas. More bunnies, matching her underpants. When you peel them off her, her hand falls between her thighs like it's always been there, and she whimpers softly. Even her whimpers are questions. You ask where her parents are while unbuttoning her blouse.

My father's dead. My stepmother killed him. And she's going to kill me.

Typical teenage fantasy, especially when they're doped up and feeling sorry for themselves. Off comes the blouse. No bra. A pause to take in the sights.

She opens her eyes to watch you watching her, though they cross with her dopey sleepiness and she closes them again. Can you protect me?

I can't protect anyone right now, kitten. I'm in deep shit and have to save my own ass first. You sound like Skipper's parrot. You used to talk only to cops and gangsters that way. Now everybody gets the same treatment. You get her pajama top on over her curly head, but she hugs the pants like a security blanket.

Please? I'm so afraid? Stay with me? Just tonight?

You've never taken advantage of dolls in distress; on the other hand, if they want to take advantage of you, your resistance is low. There's a whiskey bottle on her vanity. You pour a water glass full, savoring it as though it might be your last, thank her for it, hang your fedora on the neck of it, commence to strip down. The .45's missing. Must have left it in the street when you bumped into her. You decide to leave your trenchcoat, jacket, shirt and tie on, studs in place, in case you have to make a quick exit. The sort of exit any sane man would be making right now.

Thanks? For—? she murmurs. I don't drink whiskey? She opens her eyes blearily and sees your blond pubes, starts giggling. It's so *cute*—?

It'll grow out, you grumble, and stretch out beside her, well aware that you might be crawling into bed with a deranged killer. Well, the thrills. It's what I'm in this game for, right? you inquire of the starscaped ceiling, and, stretching out under it, you replace the hand between her legs with your own.

Game?

You wake up from a sleep so leaden you cannot think where you are until you find the dead girl beside you, strangled with her own jammies, your hand still between her legs. Ah. There's someone else in this house. Why did you assume otherwise? Sirens again, drawing up out front. This is not Blue's beat, but you wouldn't be surprised if he turned up. You are frantically hauling your pants on, stuffing your bare feet into your gumshoes, thinking fast, as fast as you can with your stunned brain. The whiskey bottle is gone, the glass, your fedora; replaced by stuffed bunnies. There must be a servants' back staircase. Your passkey worked on the front door, maybe there's another smugglers' door somewhere in the basement. You can't find the back staircase but you discover a laundry chute and you dive down it, hoping for a soft landing. Your hopes are confounded, but your stupefied senses register only the bounce. Nor does there seem to be a door that leads anywhere but to another room. You hear the thunder of heavy boots overhead. You duck into the wine cellar to hide and discover, down behind the racks, a lock set into the brick wall. Your key opens it. An irregular section of brick slides out, creating an opening just big enough to crawl through. There's a mystery here, but you're a street dick, not a metaphysician, you've no time to muse on it, they're already clattering down the basement stairs. You snatch a couple bottles of wine, sink them in your trenchcoat pockets, and you're gone, pulling the bricks closed behind you.

THIS ISN'T YOUR FIRST MAD DISHABILLE DASH OUT OF A woman's bedroom. They have mostly—your incorrigible weakness in a meaningless universe for the fleeting joys of romance—followed upon the unexpected arrival of a husband or lover, sometimes an irate parent or snapping dog, once even a crazed horse (don't ask), but it has always been your practice to leave behind hot bodies, not cold ones, the only anatomy at mortal risk generally being your own. You've had your heels and ears clipped by flying bullets, have been knocked off the sides of buildings you were scrambling down by flowerpots and birdcages, and have taken a load of buckshot in your butt—twice, same guy, same dame, going over the same back wall; learning doesn't come easy to you—but so far you have dodged the doom of so many of your clients' rivals. Those poor saps you got the goods on. The closest you've come to buying it was during a brief torrid fling with a circus aerialist with amazingly muscular jaws, one of those slim dollies who hang ninety feet above the ground by their teeth; she had oral techniques you'd never experienced before, nor have you since, and as you are always willing to take a few risks to revel in instructive marvels, you spent a lot of time between acts in her caravan, in spite of her lion-tamer husband's reputation for savagery. It wasn't easy to tear away from her mid-performance, so eventually he collared you, speaking loosely. Collar-boned you, more like. His reputation was well-deserved. First, you took a lashing from his big black whip from which you still have scars striped across your backside like a stave of music, and then you were thrown raw into the lion's cage. And this was not a lion from whose paw you'd pulled a thorn, though you did get the impression, as its lips curled back in a wet snarl, that it was laughing. Just before you could get recycled, however, you were rescued by the aerialist (another romantic) who, when the lion tamer, weary of beating her, went off for consolation from the Fat Lady, tossed the big cat a poisoned hamburger. Later, you heard, her husband got a hamburger much like it, but by then you'd stopped going to the circus.

WELL, THIS SORT OF WHAM-BAM LOVING, AS JOE THE bartender describes, approvingly, all matings, human and otherwise, has not been all of love you've known; though you always resist them, you've had tenderer feelings, too. The night the body was discovered in the docklands and then lost in the morgue, for example, you dropped by Loui's afterwards to ease the pain of a blown case and found yourself crying in your whiskey (figuratively: you don't cry) at the loss of your widow and of her remains as well. You had failed her, and having failed her, you knew then that you had loved her, and you probably said as much in your tough tight-lipped way, though they would anyway have known your true feelings by the way you blew your nose. All this was a bit too much for Joe, who started telling a dirty joke about a woman who dressed in widow's weeds to bury her broken dildo, then in white to wed her new one, but who was visited on her wedding night by the ghost of her dead dildo, accusing her of negligent dildicide. Loui laughed, interrupting the joke, which, as you knew, had as dark a punchline as any in Joe's repertoire, and said that his fourth wife, or maybe it was his fifth, used to call him, lovingly, her dildo with ears, and that she was the best wife he ever had, wives on the whole being a contentious and predatory lot.

Flame, more sympathetic, herself a sucker for impossible amours, drifted off to the floor mike and sang a song about lost love called "The Dick and the Dame." *The dick was just a trick for a dame on the game,* she moaned in her sultry voice, so full of anguish and thwarted desire. *If the chick's up shit creek, is the dick to blame . . . ?* Flame, you knew, would be happy to help you get through the night, but you needed to be alone. When she reached the last line about the dick's pursuit of the ineffable (which rhymed with "his situation was laughable"), you blew her a kiss, tugged your fedora down over your brows, lit up, and, collar up, hands in trenchcoat pockets, stepped out into the grim wet night.

The streets, wearing their heavy shadows as if dressed for a wake, were spookily abandoned except for the occasional loners hurrying along under the scattered lamps in the distance, huddled anonymously against the drizzly rain—other mourners, it seemed to you, like yourself. Cars passed but rarely and then as if without drivers or passengers, mere light dollies, interrogating the streets with their harsh probing glare. As you left Loui's upscale neighborhood and plunged into the gloomier precincts at the edge of the docklands, you found yourself wading through pools of bottomless shadow, buffeted by drifting wisps of cold emblematic fog. Like a dangerous journey into the land of the dead, as some have said. Such horseshit you don't take onboard, but you did feel your own mortality blowing foglike through you on the night and whatever you saw looked more dead than alive.

You had decided to head down to the Woodshed, known simply as the Shed, an old teapad and gutbucket often used for jam sessions, what Fingers and his chums called clambakes, and popular with ferry captains and wistful underdressed ladies past their prime. A romantic gesture. The widow, drifting in like a shadow, had found you there one night. She'd wanted to tell you another part of her story and was informed by someone that the Shed was where you could often be found. Maybe that was the night she told you about her grandfather, you don't remember. What you can't forget is the last thing she'd said: I don't even know if all this is true, Mr. Noir. I just feel I need to see you, and to do that I have to have a reason. The light picked out her hands, dragging them out of the dark. No reason needed, sweetheart, you'd assured her, and placed one hand on hers and the light there dimmed. A reason for myself, I mean, she'd said. I'm in mourning, Mr. Noir. Hesitatingly, she'd withdrawn her hand. This is not proper.

When you entered that night of the docklands murder and missing body, after your walk over from Loui's, Fingers, accompanied only by a snubnosed bassist, was riffing on an old sentimental blues ballad, a tune meant to provoke reflections upon life's brevity, and its thin sad beauty. It was late, an off night, the place was half empty. You slid into a scarred wooden booth at some remove from the drunks and ladies at the bar, but close to the little stage where Fingers was playing, tugged your fedora brim down, ordered up a double, studied the graffiti carved into the tabletop. You were one of the few who knew that Fingers got his name, not from his piano playing, but from his career as a safe-cracker. You'd once helped him beat a box job rap by convincing the District Attorney who was after him to drop the case—the D.A. was a client of a dominatrix you knew, there were photographs. Though he wasn't there that night, you'd often seen the D.A. in the Shed thereafter, and there was a rumor there was something going on between him and Fingers.

Blue has his docklands beat, Rats does, Loui his restaurant, Mad Meg her alleyways, but you have no turf of your own other than the city itself, which is to say, the indifferent world. Your bedsit's like a cheap room in some sleazy railroad hotel. Even your office is a rental and you feel like an interloper in it; if it's anyone's, it's Blanche's place. Homeless, you feel as much at home in here as anywhere, but it's not the Shed. Could be any such where. It's the beat, the melody, the melancholy, the music. You are the music while the music lasts, it says on the scarred tabletop. That sounds familiar; maybe you cut it there. You settle into these warm illusions as into an old easy chair in the front parlor, sipping the one thing that ever really tastes good to you (you're already on your third). The place itself is filthy, smoky, gloomy, rank. It's you.

When Fingers took a break you signaled with your glass to indicate you were buying him one. He hesitated, looked the other way as if not having seen you, then shrugged, nodded at the barman, picked up his drink, and came on over. He walked bent-backed, the way he sat at the piano, his drawn baggy-eyed pan announcing the end of the world. Day before yesterday. Eh, Phil-baby, howzit hangin'?

Low and twisted, Fingers. Feeling bad.

That frail in the weeds who come in here one night, the one with the sweet gams . . .

She's dead.

Yeah, I heard.

You heard? It just happened.

Word gets around. He handed you a mezzroll and you lit up. That night the widow showed up slumming here, you offered her one. She only shuddered and stared down at her hands (probably; it was dark, she was wearing her veil) and said: Please, Mr. Noir. You don't know who I am. Just as Fingers was staring now at his hands. Long bony fingers with dark yellow tobacco stains and blackened nails, hard sharp knuckles like rows of little brass studs. Sorry, man.

I was down at the morgue, Fingers. The body's gone missing. I gotta find it.

Don't do it, cat. Forget her.

Can't, Fingers, you said, sucking on your spliff. I fucked up. I owe her that much. What can you tell me?

Nuthin'. I ain't even supposed to be talkin' to you.

What do you mean, you're not supposed to talk to me? Who says?

Fingers hesitated, looked over his shoulder. A pale glow in the far corner faded away like a light being dimmed. Nobody. I just know, man.

Who's your sideman?

Don't know. Picked him up tonight.

He looks like someone smashed his face in.

Fingers grunted. That dude was born ugly, he said, getting up to go. Thanks for the jittersauce, my man. Then, holding the glass to his lips as if to finish off the drink, his bent back to the room, he growled: Check out Big Mame's.

The ice cream parlor?

He winced, as though to say, Shut up! Plant you now, dig you later, man, he declared aloud, and drifted away, tossing off a Let it wail, baby! over his shoulder.

⊙

THE NEXT DAY, EN ROUTE BIG MAME'S, YOU STOPPED in at the office to pick up another cannon, but before you could leave, Blanche brought in dossiers of three possible new clients, all lucrative, all boring. She said she was sorry about the previous client, the poor silly mixed-up thing, but she was glad all that was over. Well, you said, it's not over, and over her protests (This is a detective agency, Mr. Noir, and it is not supported by dead clients!) you stepped past her, tipping your fedora with a deadpan wink, and ankled on over to the ice cream parlor, head ducked against the blinding glare of the wet streets. There were a couple of kids in there sucking at a milkshake with two straws. The place was irritatingly cheerful and stank of milk and bubblegum. Like the morgue: sweet rot. You stared at the kids for a moment. They were blowing bubbles at each other in their shake and giggling. It was like they lived in a different world. They *did* live in a different world. It was called daytime. The parlor was otherwise empty. You could hear Big Mame at the back, ordering up bananas, nuts, and maraschino cherries. Over by the window: a table with eight or nine empty banana split bowls, one chair. You knew who'd been there. He'd left a cigar butt and a newspaper behind. You glanced at it. The usual miseries. Wars and threats of wars. Murders, robberies, crimes by the column. More rain on the way. Slumping economy. Accusations of corruption and crackdowns on juvenile troublemakers. The latest humiliating defeat of the city baseball team. Your horoscope for the day suggested that to play it safe it was better to spend the day in bed. Watch out for falling meteors, it said. Then you saw it. Bottom of page seven, the obits page: Fingers was dead. Run over by a hit-and-run driver who jumped the curb and clipped him on the sidewalk last night as he stepped out of the Woodshed.

That was when you decided to look up Rats to see what he knew about missing bodies and drive-by assassins, ended up in Skipper's sleazy waterfront den instead, got rescued from Blue's goons by Michiko and sent back to Loui's by the note she handed you.

YOU LEAN AGAINST A ROUGH WALL, LIGHT UP A FAG, THE match's flame blinding in the coalpit dark, realizing now where you'd seen before that pug-faced cabbie who delivered you to the dead sex kitten's pad: in the Shed. Fingers' ugly sideman on bass. What's the connection? No idea. Connections probably an illusion in such a fucked-up world as this. Why you're down here. Illusory connections. Until it burns your fingers, you hold the match to the wall to read the graffiti: Your future is all used up, it says. Swell. Your belly's growling, the only thing besides the scurrying vermin that breaks the silence. You've long since consumed Flame's provisions. You still have the bill clip in your pocket, but it isn't clipping anything. The big bills are gone as well and you're even out the taxi fare. Twixt twos and fews, as Fingers would say. On the nut. Sometimes you can stand up in here in the smugglers' tunnel, sometimes not. Standing or on all fours, you have to feel your way. When you pulled those bricks closed behind you, except for the basements you pass through, that was the end of any light. It's a kind of entombment, but you feel at home here, trapped in some nameless dark corner of the world and no way out, burrowing through a black night, not knowing where you're going or why, but somehow impelled to get there, the condition you were born to. The guys who built these routes must have worked their butts off. They were smalltime crooks, trying to get something for nothing, but they were heroes, too, in their way, pitting their strength and wits against the odds, and less pernicious than the grubby boiled hats on top who bully the world out of its goods, then pass laws to protect what they've stolen, hang those who try to take it back.

The impenetrable darkness reminds you of the widow. How little you knew of her. Was she just an innocent kid from the sticks who found herself helplessly drawn, through loneliness and love, into a big city plot of deceit, greed, and murder? Or was she herself, as Blanche believes, a ruthless streetwise killer, bewitchingly beautiful maybe, but all ice inside? A sexy hooker who landed a rich cokehead and bumped him off? This isn't the tender sophisticated lady you know and love, but of course her own tale addenda seemed to put the lie to her innocence. When she admitted to having been raped by her father and you said that was a rotten way to lose your cherry (there are probably nicer ways of putting it, but you don't know them; or if you know them, they don't roll out past the stones in your mouth), she confessed that her father was not her first lover, her grandfather was. She truly loved him, she said. He was so noble and handsome. He awakened dormant desires and taught her about her body. Made her feel beautiful. But which was the lie, the idyllic rural village where they sold cotton candy in the park on weekends, or the sexy grandfather? She often seemed to be crafting her confessions, if they were that, for you. As if, all along, she were trying to reach you, read you, tell you what you wanted to know. Her father, later, was in such a hurry, she said, but her grandfather was gentle and took his time. They spent a whole day just touching each part of each other's body and talking about them, without even kissing them. Who was that for, if not for you, you randy old lech? And your own attraction to her: Did it matter whether she was the abused virgin from the back country or a vicious scheming assassin? Well, it probably affected the way you'd have touched her, if she'd ever have let you: lacing fingers tenderly or grabbing her wrist with the gun in it; but, no, whatever, you were hooked. And, except for the Creep's nasty remarks and the legs she showed, you don't even know what she looked like. Although now, in the deep dark, as, crouched under the low roof, you stumble along (you can't hear your own footsteps: the walk of a dead man, as they say), you can almost see her. Smiling at you behind her veil. Sweetly. Wickedly.

And then—a thin light, a locked door that your passkey opens—you do see her. Nearly knocks you to your knees. Veiled, dressed in black, black-stockinged, standing in a mostly naked crowd. Of manikins. You're in the basement of a women's dress shop, filled with manikins and parts of manikins, one of them decked out in widow's weeds. There's a bride, too, a swimmer, a woman in jodhpurs, others in underwear or night-gowns or business suits. Most of them are bare or mostly bare, most bald as well, some half-disassem-bled, armless, headless. In the dusty penumbral light, there's an eerie sensuality about them with their angu-lar provocative poses, their hard glossy surfaces, their somnambulant masklike faces, features frozen in gla-cial eyeless gazes. In short, not unlike most of the women you've known. You know you're in trouble because they look good to you. You pass among them, stroking their sleek idealized bottoms, their hard shiny breasts. Why are they so beautiful? You peel down undies, lift skirts. Nothing underneath of course. Just a lot of rigid bare bodies, dressed in their absence of def-inition, yet, in a chilling way, they excite you. You touch the hard lumps between their legs, thinking about the soft wet pussy of the little sex kitten, the one who asked you to protect her and whom you failed, poor thing. So alive. What did the Creep say? Like wet velvet. Though he was talking about a dead woman.

Wasn't he? Or. . . . You hesitate before the manikin widow, feeling confused, chastised. Like you know something you don't know, or shouldn't. You take hold of the black skirt hem, drop it. Not right. Can't look under the veil either. You don't want to see that cold blind deadpan face.

There's a message taped to the pubic knoll of a nearby manikin, naked except for a red wig. It's from Flame. Figured you'd have to come through here sooner or later, Phil, it says. Just wanted to let you know that the cops got Rats. Collared him after he saw you. He's in for a bad time. But it's you they're really looking for. They think Rats will lead them to you. You're a famous guy. They're pinning at least five different murders on you, lover. I'm hot! And lonely without you! Be careful! I miss you, baby! I want you back!

You'd hoped Rats had got away. He was on the run, he'd put himself at risk to tell you something about what you were looking for. You'd met in a train-yard amid abandoned railroad cars black with rain, someone had apparently tipped the cops, and they were waiting for him. For you, too, probably. All Rats had time to tell you was that there was a mystery about the widow. Had to do with the chalk drawing. And then he told you to tear ass, he'd lead the cops a chase, he knew how to shake them. You got away but apparently he

didn't. Must have lost his clog, the poor gimpy fucker.
You owe him one.

WHAT YOU'D BEEN LOOKING FOR, EVER SINCE IT WAS
found down in the docklands, then disappeared, was
the widow's body, and after a couple of bad days, you
were consoled the night that Michiko's note sent you
there by Flame's own orange-tufted nicely cushioned
pubic knoll (you kiss your fingertips and tap the hard
one here in memory of it). You were in need of consolation. Your client dead, her body missing, your pal
Fingers run down, your own health in constant jeop-
ardy. Not to mention what would have been a broken
heart if you had one to break. That was a few nights
ago when you were met in Loui's by the ham-fisted
thug with the roscoe. The suit. The Hammer. You
never learned his real moniker; Flame named him that
night with her song. He quickly became something of
a nuisance. Later he got knocked off in the alley,
blown away with your own .22. According to Snark.
So who was he really? Why did he want you to lay off
the body hunt? What was he doing the next night
down at the docks? The widow had spoken of a mad-
cap brother who liked to emulate detective pulp
badguys. Could this have been the same guy? She said

she thought he was working for Mister Big, might have been out to snuff her. Going for badguy sainthood. If that was the Hammer in the alley rain, who were his killers? Rivals of Mister Big? Or Big's own hatchetmen, eliminating a cowboy interloper? Maybe Loui had some of his mob connections take him out as a favor to you. And to himself: the mug was bad for business, as he said himself that night, signaling his bouncers to toss him. Joe the bartender dismissed him as a fucked-up dude, winging it on his own, noting that real hoods, like cops, tend to partner up when on the job. And they go careful on the sauce. This guy had been in here before and didn't know when to stop. You could feel for that. You know when to stop but knowing doesn't help.

The next day you launched the search in earnest, starting with a return to Big Mame's ice cream parlor. Fingers sent you here and you asked Big Mame why. She just shook her jowls and went about her business. She had one of those classic mudbucket faces, sullen and rumpled and full of sorrow, the kind that was very expressive but said nothing.

Fingers is dead, Mame.

No blame on me, Mister Bad Luck.

There's a dame who's dead, too. A widow. Why are people trying to stop me from looking for her remains?

Can't say. What's it to you anyhow? You do the dirty with this lady?

I don't even know what she looks like.

So how you gonna know it's her if you find her?

I'll know.

But it was true. How would you know? By her legs? Legs aren't faces with eyes and noses. Good thing, too. It would be a mess to have faces down there. No, what you were in love with was something less visible: a voice, a manner, poise. Style. A counter to your cluttered and seedy life. Would that be recognizable in a dead body? Mame only folded her arms over her big breasts and stared dully at you when you asked her questions, but you figured, even on the run, Rats would have to stop by sooner or later for a hot butterscotch sundae, he couldn't stay away, so you let her know you wanted to see him. Your favorite is a five-layer parfait she makes, topped with cherry sauce, whipped cream, and rum raisins, and you had one of those before hitting the streets again.

YOU PAID FOR IT OUT OF THE ALLOWANCE BLANCHE HAD handed you earlier in the day on your way out the door, given only after you'd agreed to change your socks. Blanche seemed to be turning up at the office more regularly now that the widow was dead. Mostly to try to dissuade you from the unprofitable pursuit of a client who no longer existed. She had peered reproachfully at you over her horn-rimmed spectacles, plucking red hairs from your pants and jacket and unshaved lip, and pointed out that the important thing was not where the body was, but why did it go missing? In whose interest was that?

I don't know. Mister Big wanted it as a souvenir?

You are a silly man, Mr. Noir. As we know, the deceased's husband willed the estate to the two of them with the stipulation that the estate remain intact, so before it can be finally probated, one of the two beneficiaries must relinquish their share or die. The last thing the second beneficiary would want would be to lose the corpus delicti.

So I'm doing him a favor if I find it.

You might as well ask for a commission. Unless there is something wrong with the body.

What could be wrong with it?

She'd shrugged her little dismissive shrug, pushing her glasses further up her nose. Shall I cancel the ad for the miniature soldiers? Nothing's come of it. It's a waste of money.

No, constable, we have not yet abandoned the field, you'd replied, taking back your trenchcoat which she had threatened to send to the cleaners. Let's add

that we can also offer a set of miniature camp followers. Action figures. Hold down the fort, sweetheart. I'm
off to the hunt.

$$\odot$$

So, squeezing the webby black veil in your
pocket as though to wring knowing itself from it, you
pushed off from Big Mame's, your chin sticky with
cherry sauce, to see what you could turn up. For awhile,
you were literally looking everywhere, as though the
corpse might be hidden under a carpet or behind the
door. In flophouses, movie theaters, beer halls, public
toilets, penny arcades, massage parlors, gambling dens,
hock shops, gyms, and boxing arenas. You checked in
with your contacts among the city's dealers, strippers
and street vendors, numbers runners, hoods and hookers, pimps, plastic surgeons, pickpockets, addicts,
medics and ambulance drivers, counterfeiters, cops and
con artists. There were vague rumors, they wanted to
help, eager for your coin, but you got nothing you
could call a real lead. A one-armed taxi driver said he
picked up a woman dressed in black who had to be
lifted into his hack by the two gorillas she was with and
taken to a fancy block near the harbor, but added that
she snored like a horse the whole way, so that was
probably not who you were looking for. A newspaper

vendor outside the bus station who had lost his nose in the last war and had to tape his thick glasses to his temples told you he'd seen a fat guy shoving a duffelbag that might have held a body into one of the baggage lockers. You weren't sure how he could see anything through his thick ink-smudged lenses, but coughed up the better part of Blanche's allowance to get the station manager to open all the lockers within the vendor's view. There was actually a duffelbag in one of them. It was full of candy bars, jawbreakers, bubblegum, all-day suckers, and children's underwear. You'd just helped solve some crimes you'd never get credit for, might now even be accused of, but you hadn't come closer to finding the dead widow.

At the morgue, you took a look at Fingers' cadaver, stretched out flat, his hunched slump ironed out by the spine-crushing blow he took, the poor bastard. Yesterday after leaving Big Mame's, you'd stopped by the Woodshed to pay your respects. No chalk figure drawing of the victim on the sidewalk, only a bass clef like a fetus. They told you he'd been struck by a stolen taxi. The Shed's old wooden door sits back from the street. The car that decked him had to have all four wheels on the sidewalk—and, the direction it was going, would have had to cut over from the far lane. The owner shrugged and said people had different musical tastes. He knew there were some who thought Fingers was too heavy on the left hand. You asked the Creep to see all the female stiffs and made him pull them out just far enough that you could look at the legs, more in blind hope than with any conviction you'd see anything you recognized, having to put up all the while with the Creep's evil sniggering. I have some other pretty people here if there's something particular you want, he whispered, and you popped him one, right on the honker, flattening it to a bloody splatter in the middle of his ugly bug-eyed face. Made you feel better, the way hitting out always does, even if it's completely senseless. You don't understand this need for rough stuff. It's just something you have to do from time to time to tell the world what you think of it. Blanche is always telling you to grow up and stop hitting people, but you can't help it, your fists have a mind of their own, you go on doing it. You might say it's who you are, but you don't know who the fuck you are. Just a dumb dick, sometimes full of aimless rage. After you slapped the Creep around a bit more, he admitted he'd heard about a body floating around with a price tag on it, but he didn't know where it was. What do you mean, floating? I don't know, he sniveled, lapping at the blood on his upper lip. That's what I heard. You don't want me to hit you again, do you, Creep? He rolled his popeyes up at you and grinned with swollen lips, his nose streaming. Yes, please. You left the sick sonuvabitch and stepped out into the night.

Where it was raining again. Lightly, just enough to scatter glittery reflections on the street and to drive most pedestrians inside, making the streets seem like a damp empty stage with sinister events brewing in the darkened wings. You pulled your fedora down over your eyes, doggedly continuing your search, stopping in at the aquarium, casino, the Chinese theater. On the third floor of a cheap hotel in the theater district, a silhouetted woman was undressing behind a drawn blind. Same window as last night? No, different neighborhood. The kind of movie showing nightly all across town. The movie you're in. Chasing shadows. You paused to look into a backstreet watch-repair shop window. Old sleuth's habit of using a window as a mirror to see if anyone's following you. There was. Fat Agnes. Across the street. You spun around to confront him: not there. Just a blinking neon light advertising McGinty's Pool Hall. You turned back to the window to check: Yes, that's all it was. You were on edge. Seeing things. What you saw now through the curtain of rain dripping off your hat brim was your own reflection, staring back at you with rain-curtained eyes, cigarette glowing at the lips, the multitudinous faces of time ticking away in the shadowy background. What are you doing out here, you dumb fuck, you asked it, it asked you, the lit cigarette bobbing as if scribbling out your question. You don't love the widow, alive or dead. That's bullshit. You don't love anyone, wouldn't know what to do if you did. This is what you love. The gumshoe game. Played alone on dark wet streets to the tune of the swell and fade of car horns, sirens, the sounds of breaking glass, cries in the street, the percussive punctuation of gunshots and shouted obscenities. You nodded and your reflection nodded. You love your own bitter misery, your knotted depression. In short, you're a fucking romantic, Noir, as Joe the bartender likes to say. A disease you medicate with booze, needing a dose now. The widow knew how to get under your skin. Denial. Frustration. Deception. Depravity. You eat it up.

Cheered by all this heavy thinking, you crossed over to McGinty's, where you found Cueball alone at table, peering down the length of his cue the way he used to peer down rifle barrels, his eyes so close together they seemed almost to join at the bridge of his sharp narrow nose, crossing into each other as they took aim. He wasn't always Cueball. He was once a famous hit man named Kubinsky, but he changed his name while doing time when nature changed his hair style, leaving him with a shiny white dome like one of these wigless manikins. About as much emotion in him, too. Give him a pistol, he'd somehow shoot himself in the elbow, but put a rifle in his hands and the flies on the wall ducked and shielded their eye facets. No telling how

many poor suckers he'd iced before his prison voca-
tional retraining. When he was still Kubinsky and had
hair, it was said he worked on occasion for Mister Big
and you asked him what he knew about the man. You
were convinced that the elusive Big had something to
do with the killing of the widow and probably the disappearance of the body, too, in spite of what Blanche
said. Yeah, I done some jobs for him, I think they were
for him, Cueball said, potting three balls with one
stroke, but I never seen him. There was a bunch of guys
running around town saying they was Mister Big, but
none of them really was, none I met. He was quietly
clearing the table on his own, there being few who
dared challenge him. Cueball, like most professional
killers, was a loner. No male friends and, when in need,
he hung out mostly with working girls, partnered up
with none of them. Except one.

YOU KNOW THE STORY BECAUSE KUBINSKY HIRED YOU
to find and tail the girl. In Kubinsky's case it wasn't just
the fee. He was a scary client and refusing him in those
days was a kind of suicide. The chick was a dishy but
simple taxi dancer named Dolly, who confused the guys
she danced with by falling passionately in and out of
love with each of them from dance to dance, resulting

in a lot of consequential mayhem between suitors. Kubinsky was not a dancer, he literally had two left feet, the little toe on his flat archless right bigger than the big; this was not how they met. He was hired by a smalltime racketeer named Marko, one of her baffled lovers, to kill her. Marko was instructed to walk her out onto the street for a smoke between dances and he could have the pleasure of watching her drop at his feet. When Kubinsky got her in his sights, however, he was for the first time in his life utterly and hopelessly smitten. He was not confused. He knew exactly what he wanted. It was Marko took the hit just as he was fitting the fag he'd lit from his own into Dolly's lips, a cruel expectant smirk on his mug.

This ruthless cold-blooded torpedo stunned by love was a sight to see. You'd only heard about lovers drooling. Kubinsky drooled. He panted. His eyes lost focus, the pupils floating haphazardly away from the bridge of his nose. His stony white face was puffy and flushed. He stumbled when he walked, bumped into things. He wept, he snuffled, he dribbled at the crotch. You witnessed this transformation because he turned up at your office one morning, offering you a bag of money and lifetime impunity from a bump-off if you would find the missing Dolly for him and tell him what she was doing. After knocking off Marko, he'd put the rush on her immediately, walking onto the dance floor and shoving her current partner aside, which naturally impressed her, but since he was no dancer, it was not easy for Dolly to love him, open to the general idea though she always was. He'd bought up every dance night after night and did his best to learn the two-step, and finally she did seem to fall for him, enough anyway to go on a two-step tour of several exotic cities with him until the money ran out and Kubinsky had to come back and take on more contracts to pay for his love life.

The cop who had been assigned the Marko murder case, however, was waiting for her. He had figured out that to get what he wanted from her it was best if she was in love with him, which simply meant dancing with her. He booked one entire night when Kubinsky was out working and took her home with him, dancing all the way. Or, rather, as you soon learned, to a rented room across town. After a couple of days, his wife reported him missing. Probably he'd forgotten what it was he'd wanted to know. You submitted your report. Kubinsky returned, asked for all copies, plus negatives of the damning photos and your notebooks. His eyes were crowding the bridge of his nose once more, though redder than usual. The pallor was back. His rifle case was in hand. He seemed to be a doing a melancholic little two-step there in the doorway. He said he planned to eat the barrel of his rifle, but first he had some business to attend to. Crossing Kubinsky could be lethal, but you'd had something going with Dolly for a dance or two yourself, and wanted to know she was still there for a dime. Besides, Kubinsky was a man of his word; you figured he'd honor his warranty. You tipped the cops.

Kubinsky was nabbed before the killing, which no doubt embittered him, but it saved him from the chair. The cop changed his name and disappeared. So did Dolly. Maybe they're dancing together yet. Did Cueball né Kubinsky ever figure out who ratted on him? Maybe. But prison transformed him. Maybe it was the saltpeter in his diet. Most likely it was his new obsession. Without a rifle at hand, he picked up a cue stick in the prison rec room and the rest is poolhall history.

CUEBALL HAD A STRAIGHT SHOT ON THE SIX-BALL INTO the corner, but he chose instead to go for a double bank, clipping the six from behind the eight just enough to send it skidding into the same corner, the cue ball continuing up the table and nudging the seven-ball into a side pocket. You wondered if he ever attempted any ricochet hits that way. Two for the price of one. I heard about a floating body, Cuby. You hear anything?

Word's getting around you're shit luck on a smelly fork, Noir.

That scare you, Cuby?

He shrugged, chalking up. It'll cost you.

Here's what I got. You emptied out your pockets onto the green nap.

Down at the docks, he said. Pier four. Somebody's boat. Won't come cheap. Better reload before you go down there.

YOU'RE HUNGRY, WISH YOU HADN'T POLISHED OFF Flame's sandwiches and whiskey so fast. You search the women's dress shop basement for provisions, poking through the wardrobes, disassembling some of the manikins. Sorry, sweetheart, I'm going to have to take your head off, you won't need it. You feel like some kind of hardnosed gynecological sawbones, watched by a widow rigid with disapproval. You find hollow limbs and heads and molded bellybottoms full of stash left behind by the smugglers—bags and bricks of narcotics, stolen jewels, watches, banded stacks of bills no doubt from bank heists—but nothing to eat. Money's sometimes called lettuce; you try it, it's not lettuce. You pick up a loose forearm with a screw at the elbow end for attachment to the rest of the arm, and use it to pull the

cork on one of the bottles of wine in your trench pockets. They're both from some country you've never
heard of called Bordox. Sounds like an antacid or a
cleansing agent. Tastes like one, too. You shake the
bottle. It's full of gunk. The stuff's well past it. You like
your wine straight from the grape. You can add the
alcohol yourself. But you're hungry and thirsty and it
goes down easily, straight from the neck. You strip the
bride and use her white wedding gown as a blanket, tip
the widow to the floor and cuddle up beside her under
it, the forest of plastic bodies towering above you.

While you're lying there, Mister Big turns up,
wanting to see the advertised camp followers, and, having nothing else to offer, you point up at the manikins.
He laughs what seems to you a cruel laugh. You're a
sucker for dangerous dames, Noir, he says. He has
brought along an army of antique mobsters. Knights,
archers, crossbowmen. Or perhaps these are the miniature soldiers you are trying to sell him. Probably. Though
they are not miniature, they are life-size, unless you and
he are toy-size. They are blind and motionless, yet somehow threatening, like momentarily paralyzed zombies.
You feel some elemental boundary has been breached.
You cling to the widow for reassurance. But it is not the
widow, she has disappeared again; the manikin lying
beside you is naked and tattooed like Michiko and she
has pushed her leg between your legs. It is snowing

cocaine and diamonds from above. The stuff would seem to be leaking out from between the pink shiny thighs of the giant manikins, but this is a mystery, for there are no outlets there. Maybe this is what Big was laughing at. He has made a joke about plastic surgery while wielding an ice pick. You are trying to figure things out, Noir, he says, when there is nothing to figure. You try to look closely at him so you'll remember his face, but he is never quite where you look. Out of the corner of your eye you see him trying on the bride's gown. This excites the tattooed manikin beside you who has grabbed your dick with a cold dead claw. Which is how you wake up, spilling your seed into the widow manikin's inflexible hand and scared shitless.

You need a john, can't find one, use a hollow leg. The widow manikin lies on her back at your feet like a stiffened corpse, her hand held palm-up accusingly as if you might have killed her with your spunk. You need to get out of here. The only door in sight other than the one you came in by needs your passkey and leads back into the tunnels.

BY THE LIGHT OF DAY, SPEAKING LOOSELY (IT'S BUTTHOLE black in here), your dream makes depressing sense to you. After buying Cueball's tip a couple of nights ago, just before you had to go underground, you headed straight for the fogged-in docklands and pier four. Your pockets were empty except for the widow's veil and note, but you were holstered up with other tools of the trade. Marketing corpses was still illegal, far as you knew; you figured you could just lay claim to it, at gunpoint if necessary, throw it over your shoulder and tote it away.

It was a dark damp night, the sort you're most at home in, with a thick coiling fog that concealed movement and allowed only occasional glimpses of wet brick, swaying yellow lamps, occasional gray shadowy figures emerging out of and disappearing into the mist. Such fleeting glimpses (for a moment you caught sight of the sky-blue police building spectrally aglow as if lit from within, and then as quickly it was gone again) were like the sudden brief insights that cut through the fog of a case, and you were on the alert for anything that might help you solve the mystery of your client's life and death and her hold on you. You were trying to fit the bits together, but they were invisible bits—it was like trying to work a jigsaw puzzle without the pieces. As you drew nearer to the piers, warning signs appeared saying WATCH YOUR STEP and DANGER—HIGH VOLTAGE, and it was as though they were posted there for you. Things Blanche might say. You could hear water slapping softly against something. The honk of unseen gulls. Must be close. But which was pier four? No idea. You heard heavy footfalls behind you and ducked behind a small white fishbait hut with shutters on the windows, a ramp at the door, a box outside with the sign: ICE. Which you read as: *freeze!* A burly mug in polished dogs stomped by, head down, muttering to himself. Big guy with big mitts. On a hunch, you let him pass, then stepped out into the fog and followed him. More by ear than eye.

At the water's edge, you passed huge coils of black cable on massive bobbins like giant spools of thread, beached buoys and floats, old concrete gas tanks standing together like benumbed sentries, wreathed by wisps of fog as if they were smoking (you could have used one). You proceeded warily, stopping whenever the steps stopped. They backtracked sometimes, suggesting the guy you were following didn't know where he was going either. Or maybe he had heard you behind him and was checking or else was just pacing. Forced you to flatten yourself against shed walls from time to time. Then their sound changed. They were walking on wood, growing fainter. Then they stopped. You crept forward, found the wooden pier, stepped out on it stealthily. Foghorns in the distance. The squawking gulls. Buoy bells. The black water lapping. Otherwise a thick misty silence. If the guy knew you were there, he could be on you before you could see him. Blackness at first, but then a hollow glow ahead, which eventually revealed itself as a ghostly white yacht, rearing up in the fog. There was something nightmarish about it, but you didn't hesitate. You boarded it, .22 in hand.

Was there someone else on the yacht? There was. Through a small window, you could see a light moving about down in the main cabin. Probably that tough you were tailing. The light was picking out leather sofas, teak tables and cabinets, navigation charts, fish tackle, step boxes. And then he saw it, you saw it, in the adjoining bunkroom, half obscured by a bead curtain: a body. He moved toward it (there was something glinting in his free hand), and you moved toward the cabin door. It was ajar. As you slipped through it, the guy doused his flashlight and turned on the bedside lamp and you saw then who he was. The bum you'd met the night before in Loui's. The suit. The Hammer. And by the hothouse aroma you knew whose body it was. It also belonged to someone you'd seen the night before. She'd helped you escape Blue's goons at Skipper's. You'd heard her scream. You thought about just backing out and leaving them to it, but then you saw the Hammer raise a knife, and you stepped quietly forward, tapped him on the shoulder, and when he spun around, met him with a roundhouse, gat in hand. He crumpled like a sack of shit. You grabbed up the shiv, tossed it out the porthole, and while he was still groggy, you lifted him by his collar and slugged him again. And again. Did this palooka work for Mister Big? Take that, Mister Big! *Wham!* Was he responsible for Michiko's death? Take that—*pow!*—for Michiko. The widow's disappearance? *Biff! Bam!* There was a telephone on the bedside table. You ripped it out of the wall and hit him over the head with it, then clobbered him with a brass telescope. You were having a great time. You lifted him for one last blow to the gut (his jaw was hurting your knuckles) and threw what was left of the rube to the floor, went over to kiss the "4" on Michiko's cold forehead. Goodnight, sweetheart, you said. Phil-san gonna miss you, baby. You strode off the yacht, lighting up, feeling pretty good about yourself. Until he caught up with you.

YOU CAME AROUND, STRETCHED OUT IN YOUR BRUISED skin on your office sofa, Blanche applying ice packs and iodine and spooning in a bit of what she called cough medicine. Something you'd picked up from Rats for moments like this. There was nothing that did not hurt. Every time we get up, something comes along and knocks us on our ass again. As someone said. One of your clients maybe. Laughing probably. Just before he got knocked down for good.

Lift your leg, Mr. Noir.

Ow!

Now the other one.

Oh shit. What happened?

You tell me, Mr. Noir. They fished you out of the water down at the docks, badly damaged. Your friend Officer Snark saw the light on and dropped you off up here rather than hand you over to Captain Blue, who I believe harbors bad feelings toward you.

It was the goddamned Hammer, you groaned. He hit me when I wasn't looking.

The Hammer?

A guy I ran into last night. The one who told me to lay off the search for the body. I should have killed the bastard. I don't know if I'm tough enough for this racket, Blanche. But what are you doing here? It's after midnight.

After the new advertisement, the calls just kept coming in. Some of them were not nice. I have finally had to take the phone off the hook. Either we cancel that ad, Mr. Noir, or I quit.

Sure, sweetheart. Kill it. I don't think I want to find that evil fat-assed sonuvabitch anyway. Or the body either. Leave it lie. Wherever.

I am pleased to hear it, Mr. Noir. If you had listened to me in the first place, this wouldn't have happened.

Your clothes were drenched and filthy and in dire need of mending. I'll bring them back in the morning. Then we'll close this case once and for all. Is there anything more I can . . . ?

Well, I could use a good brandy, but—

There's a bottle on the table beside you, Mr. Noir. I took the precaution . . .

Beautiful. You're an angel, angel.

She blushed, took her glasses off for a moment, put them on again. I try to do my best, Mr. Noir. Now get some rest and take care of yourself. You shouldn't be disturbed. The phone is disconnected and I'll doublelock the door.

Thanks, kid. And hit the lightswitch when you go.

A FEW BRANDIES LATER, YOU WERE STILL ON YOUR BACK, but back on the case again, thinking about your client, her story. On the one hand, she seemed to have been a ruthless schemer who twisted men and truths around her little finger like taffy, and on the other, a sweet kid from a nice town with a weakness for older guys. You, for instance. Not Blanche's view, but then Blanche trusted no one. Made her a useful assistant in a detective agency but blinded her to life's tenderer side. That night, lying there in pain and darkness (this is a tough

life), the cough medicine just beginning to take a numb-
ing grip, was when you first started thinking about the
way the widow might have been using her old-guys stories as a way of coming on to you. I was strangely flattered by the heartrending ardor of his gaze when he
looked at me, she said of her grandfather, or else her
father. While gazing steadily at you through her veil
(you supposed), her thighs whispering. I felt an eager
affection coming from him, melting my resolve. My
heart jolted and my pulse pounded. I knew it wasn't
right, but I was powerless to resist. It was the most
important experience of my life, Mr. Noir. But not
always older guys. There was that football player in her
home town, her first sweetheart, the stud she romped
with on the village bandstand. You once asked her
whatever happened to him. It is unkind of you, Mr.
Noir, to keep bringing up embarrassing moments from
the past, she said. If you continue, I will have to be less
candid with you. But if you must know, my father had
a man-to-man talk with him over a new drink he had
concocted in his laboratory. My father was always
a great experimenter. Perhaps my sweetheart overin-
dulged. He awoke several hours later less a man than
he was before.

When was it she told you this? In the Shed? Here
in the office? Maybe the night she picked you up on the
street when you were in trouble. You'd just come out of

the Vendome after meeting with that guy in the goatee who wanted to buy the toy soldiers, Marle, one of Mister Big's lieutenants, you'd assumed, and had started down the mostly empty street. You'd paused to light up, and noticed there was a little cluster of men huddled in the shadows just beyond the next streetlamp. Others, you sensed, were gathering behind you. You touched your rod, looking around for some place to throw yourself if the bullets started to fly, when a limousine screeched up to the curb. The back door flew open: it was the widow. Get in, Mr. Noir. Quickly. You needed no second invitation. Bullets were zinging off the limo's roof even as you sped away. What was that all about? she asked as though somewhat exasperated. I think I'm on to something, you said. You couldn't help but notice that her black skirt had hiked up a bit when she leaned over to open the door, revealing a tiny patch of pale flesh just above the gartered black stocking. Since she didn't pull the skirt back down you thought tonight might be the night. The driver was a hulk who didn't talk, though there was something stiff-necked about him that suggested an inner rage, or else a humorless stupidity. You filled her in on the miniature soldiers scheme, she told you family stories. You remembered that at some point she said: My body melted against his and the world was filled with him. A golden wave of passion and love flowed between us.

Was that the football player? Her husband? Or maybe she was defending her father after some disparaging remark you'd made. The sacredness of family: one of her themes. Might even have been her brother. Any of whom other than the dead husband may have been driving the limo. My body began to vibrate with liquid fire, she said. You figured this was an open invitation but knew better than to throw yourself on her and rip her clothes off, as was your wont. Even trying to touch her knee or that bare patch which you couldn't stop staring at would be rebuffed, you knew. You had to hope you were headed to her place where all would be revealed. But she dropped you off in front of your office building and said good night, the liquid fire abruptly quenched. Or dammed. What do you do with liquid fire? You were in some pain and about to slam the door in reply, when she reached out her hand, took yours, and squeezed it gently in her warm moist palm. Had the same effect as if she'd squeezed your dick. When all this is over, she said, her voice trailing off into some limitless future. And then she was gone. That was the last night you saw her alive.

You were still hurting, but the edge was off, blunted by Rats' prescription, the brandy, and the flow of blood to other parts. Recalling the widow's stories had filled your dick with a bit of liquid fire of its own and, lying there on the office sofa, you had taken it in

hand. You were changing the story. You weren't rip-
ping her clothes off, she was. She was mad with desire,
couldn't wait. Neither could you. Nevertheless you fell
asleep. You don't remember what you dreamt, but
when you woke you thought you were locked in that
fishbait hut at the docks and couldn't get out. There
was someone in the office. Over near the hall door.
More than one. Where's the fucking flashlight, one of
them asked. I forgot it, Marle. Shall I turn on the
lights? No, you goddamn idiot. Light a match. Seemed
to be several of them, all bumping into each other,
cursing softly. Your heater was in your trenchcoat
pocket, hanging from a clothes tree near the door.
What you still held in your hand was useless. Fishbait.
Where do you think the snoop's stowed them little
fuckers, Marle? Start with the desk. I'll look for a wall
safe. Dibs on one a them camp followers if we find
them. You slid softly off the sofa onto the floor for
maximum cover. The only thing close at hand was the
brandy bottle. You took a final slug, hating to waste it,
then pitched it toward one of the struck matches. He
hit me, Marle! one of them screamed. They started
shooting. Bullets were flying. One struck the sofa
where you'd been lying with a muffled thud. Oh shit!
He got me! It's an ambush, Marle! There's hundreds of
'em! They—*aaargh!* All their guns were blazing at
once. It was like the finale of a fireworks display.

There were screams, curses, crashing bodies. The shattering of glass.

When silence had fallen, you crept over to get your rod, throw on the lights. There were five dead guys in leather jackets. May have been more. The door was open and there was a trail of blood out into the hallway. Was Marle among the late departed? Probably. Three of them had goatees, more than you'd seen before in the whole city. You felt good. It was as if you'd accomplished something. It relaxed you and you locked the door and doused the lights and crashed to the sofa again, falling almost immediately into the sweetest deepest sleep you'd enjoyed since the widow first turned up. Certainly nothing like it since.

BY THE TIME BLANCHE WOKE YOU THE NEXT MORNING with your mended and freshly ironed clothes, she had already cleaned up the mess. Except for a few new pockmarks in the walls and furniture freshly stressed by ricocheting bullets, the place looked like it always did. Good thing, too, because Blue turned up while you were still shaving. He'd traced the phone number in the ad and wanted to see your miniature soldiers.

You're not going to believe this, Blue, but they were rented, photographed, and returned.

You're right, Noir, I don't believe it. Who'd you return them to, the man you rented them from?

A guy who said he was his brother.

Sure, tell me another. They've been stolen, Noir, and you're the last guy to have seen them. I'm putting you under arrest.

Sounds like an insurance scam, Blue. You're playing right into the hands of the real crooks. Blue only smiled. You knew you were in for a working over by Blue and his goons down at the station. But you'd just had a working over, you didn't need another one.

Then Blanche went over and whispered something in Blue's ear, winked at you past the back of his head.

You mean—? Yeah, good point. All right, Noir. I'm gonna let you go for the moment. But I'll be keeping an eye on you.

What did you tell him? you asked her after the captain had left.

That it was your birthday, Mr. Noir, and that he should come back tomorrow.

My birthday's not until six months from now.

There was a phone call for you while you were sleeping. From somebody's ice cream parlor. She wants you to stop by. Have you been going off your diet again, Mr. Noir?

At Big Mame's you had another parfait. Why not.

With hot butterscotch, maraschino cherries, and marshmallows on top. Instead of a chocolate twig sticking out, there was a rolled-up note from Rats asking you to meet him in the railway freight yard near the grain elevator at sundown. Sundown? That thing still came up?

⊙

Now, as you have a smoke and polish off the second bottle of wine from its shattered neck, slumped against a wall in the smugglers' tunnel, remembering with nostalgia Big Mame's parfaits and meditating morosely on the thready web of story you've become entangled in, it occurs to you that the tattoo on your butt has stopped itching. Maybe that means they're finally leaving you alone. Though who's "they"? Trouble with webs. When you're in one, you can't see past the next knot. It's like being trapped in two dimensions, cut off from overviews. Not something achievable from down here, but maybe you can get an underview. Look up destiny's skirts. That old whore. Very dark under there, as always. Like the city. Oozing with slime and enshrouded in fog. Something nosing around your pantleg. You give it a kick. You feel headachy and rumpled, dirty, your sockless feet sweaty in your shoes. How long have you been down here? Weeks maybe.

Time passes indifferently in the shapeless dark—or near dark, as the case now is: You've crawled from a pitch blackness into a dim gray light coming from you know not where. Or else you've dozed off and it has crept up on you in your stupor. The weed's not your brand, but it will have to do. Down to the last one, though, the deck's empty. What you've had instead of food. You spit out the chip of glass between your teeth, toss the bottle aside, tuck the fag end in the corner of your mouth, and, on hands and knees, press on grimly toward whatever's ahead.

What you find is another low locked door, light leaking thinly around the edges, and the first thing you hear when you unlock it and stick your nose in is: I'll tell, I'll tell! Don't hit me again! and you know where you are: the basement of Blue's docklands police station. You've been here before as a guest, leaving a tooth behind to cover room and board. You back out quietly, but what choice do you have? It's through here to the next door, if there is one and this isn't a dead end, or crawl back to the strangled sex kitten's pad, where they're probably still hunting for you. Wouldn't last long there. So, hoping that the element of surprise might give you an edge, you push on through and rise up with a snarl, legs apart, fists in trenchcoat pockets as though clenching iron, smoldering butt dangling from your lower lip. Two guys in white shirts are beating up a prisoner in the holding cell under a harsh light, three others are sitting at a table under a hanging lamp with a green shade, smoking, playing cards. Snark is there with a pack in his hand, wearing his leather shoulder holster over his black suspenders, elastic bands around his shirt sleeves, sucking on a whiskey bottle. They ignore you, don't even seem to see you there. It's like you're invisible; or they've agreed you are. They may have a rule about it. Some deal struck with the smugglers. Rats once hinted at it. The place has a closed old-socks smell like a gym, the cement floor stained darkly. The cops at the table holler at the other two to get back to the game. Their prisoner has passed out, so, with a final kick to the belly, they shrug and do so, leaving the cell door ajar, probably hoping he'll try to escape and they can shoot him. A new hand is dealt, bills and coins are tossed toward the pot at the center.

You go over and poke around in their lunchboxes, find half a baloney sandwich and a candybar. Snark, his thumbs in his suspenders, is talking about you. He says you've been a busy boy, you're the prime suspect in at least five murders, maybe more. Possible pedophilia on top of it. Blue, he says, couldn't be happier. On the table beside him is your fedora. He puts it on (it sits on his big head like a party hat) and says he doesn't think you're guilty, but tough shit, you'll probably get the chair anyway. The others laugh, smoke around their ears like smutty halos, and Snark grunts, his equivalent of a laugh. Foo. The Bordox hasn't settled well on your empty stomach. Which is in sudden turmoil. A cleansing agent, after all, the candybar the fatal catalyst. Snark is laying out the evidence against you, which could be useful, but you're headed, on the double, for the john, the porcelain appurtenance you need so badly on bare bulb-lit view behind its gaping door.

Shoot-outs and drive-by killings on city streets, hold-up victims gunned down behind their counters, mob hits in restaurants, these are the images that captivate the public, but they are all far down the crime-scene frequency list behind beds and biffies. Your getting the goods on an adulterous lover has usually led to blood on the tiles and linens. Political wheeler-dealers and mob bosses are rarely snuffed with their dignity intact. Michiko once told you about a lover, poisoned in effect by a powerful laxative in his wasabi and killed when he heaved himself desperately onto a booby-trapped stool. Your clients often ask you for your targets' toilet habits. The poopoo charts, as Blanche calls them, wrinkling her nose in disdain, though she knows and

accepts the importance of the body's habits and exuda-
tions in committing and solving crimes, and has
often, in her own prim manner, schooled you in their
finer points.

Gazing morosely out at the crumpled body in the
holding cell from your disheartening squat over the
seatless crapper, you notice the black-on-black door
with its silver lock at the back of the cell, and now,
after wiping yourself with the crime reports nailed to
the wall for the purpose, you pull up your pants and
stride toward it, wary eye on the card players. Who are
in a distracting row about an extra ace on the table, fingers pointed at Snark. Any stupid beast on the run
knows better than to step into a cage with a lure at the
back, but it's your only shot, and when the cell door
does not spring shut behind you, you're figuring you
just might make it. Until the prisoner on the floor of the
cell grabs your ankle, making you nearly drop the key.
You kick free, cursing him silently, but see then it's your
old chum Rats. The poor sonuvabitch is still wearing
his special shoe but they have rammed it onto the
wrong foot. Since you got Flame's note, taped to the
manikin, you've worried that you might have been set
up, used as a decoy by the cops to nab both of you in
one swoop. Why else did Blue let you go? You know
trying to carry Rats out with you will break the invisi-
bility spell in here, but he's a pal and you owe him one,

what can you do. You unlock the black door with your passkey (yes, it works!), prop it open, and step behind it for a moment, take a deep breath, then dash back and grab up the lifeless backstreet merchant, toss him over your shoulder. You hear a phone ring somewhere. And then the bullets start flying, ricocheting off the bars, whizzing past your head. You pocketed some of the manikin stash and now throw loose bills and a bunch of bags and bindles out the door as you duck back into it to keep the avaricious fuckers busy while you make your getaway.

Mankind's absurd fate, you are reminded as you stagger along, pushing deeper into the smugglers' passage, the shooting and footsteps behind you dying away, is slow suffocation on a sick and dying planet: the tunnel is apparently linking up to the city's sewer system and the air is getting decidedly pungent. The species of which you are a dissolute member does not live, it endures, and this is what it smells like. Rats weighs a ton and you wonder if they, literally, pumped him full of lead. Where the tunnel opens up into the sewers, you have a choice: which direction? Old rule: follow the flow. But further downstream, you run into multiple branches. It may be just glitter off the wet walls, but you seem to catch a glimpse of Fat Agnes and you start to splash along behind him, but at the fork you spy an old tennis ball, speared by a swizzle stick, in the mouth of the other branch. It's your princess of the alley. Someone still loves you. The teasing will-o'-the-wisp glow of Fat Agnes continues to appear down one cloacal channel or another as you proceed, but Mad Meg's buttons, shoelaces, tennis balls, and candy wrappers lead you out at last.

You emerge from the pipe through which the city's sewage is dumped into the sea. You drop Rats on a pile of stones and concrete chunks and wade out into the water to wash the sludge off your shoes and pantlegs. Out here, the air stinks of rotting fish and rusting metal, but it's a relatively sweet stink and you suck it in. The gulls are squawking, protesting at your walking through their dinner. It's some dark time of day which around here could be noon. You can hear the rhythmic growl of unseen traffic, an echoey medley of sirens, horns. The way they sound off the water: early evening maybe. There's a ferry parked nearby, its carport open. You've seen that before, know where you are. Skipper's lowlife hooch house is not far away. Place to lie low for a time. First, you put Rats' shoe with the three-inch heel on the right foot, and while you're doing that he comes around. His scarred lips move. He seems to be trying to tell you something. You lean close. Flame, he whispers. Flame? He's out again.

You heave the old grifter back up on your shoulders and trudge toward Skipper's, planning to use

what's left of your manikin stash as currency to hole
out there until this blows over, even if you have to wait
until Blue retires from the force. On the way, you pass
the place where the body was found. The trigger for the
mess you're in. The chalk drawing has washed away,
replaced by a crude sketch of a naked guy with a big
pistol for a dick, firing away at a disembodied cunny
hanging in the air like a worm-eaten apple. Nothing
left of the original crime scene portrait but a pale col-
ored smudge underneath the pistol. You gaze down at
it, trying to remember how it was when you first saw
it. You do remember. Oh man. Who can you trust? You
drop Rats off at Skipper's with a packet of the smugglers' C-notes, pick up some fags, and, head buried in
your turned-up collar, head for Loui's.

ALL OVER TOWN AS YOU WALK THROUGH IT, YOUR MUG
glowers darkly on WANTED posters. They'll never recognize you. You're prettier than that. Something wrong
with the picture, though. What is it? You put yourself
in Blanche's shoes. Well, for one thing, you're wearing
a fedora on the poster, Mr. Noir, and you don't have
that any more. And there's no folded handkerchief in
your jacket breast pocket. That's not even your pinstripe suit. Blanche thinks you're too unobservant for a

private dick. She likes to set little tests for you, moves things around in the office, adds an ornament to your desk, hangs a new picture, paints the walls a different color, then asks you what's changed. The only thing you ever notice is if she moves the sofa because when you go to lie down on it you hit the floor. You use the forest-and-trees argument: when you're on a case, you're focused, see what's important, but too many details are irrelevant and clutter your vision. She says there are no forests, that's a false and undefinable category, there are only trees. When you described the chalk drawing to her, she wanted to know if you could see the victim's ears. You didn't remember but said probably not, why did she ask? The outlined body you described, Mr. Noir, was a naked one. Your client was never naked, but men like to draw women that way. So, unless it was somebody else like one of your waterfront floozies, you can ignore everything about the drawing from the neck down. But men are never interested in women's heads and would just draw what they saw. So, was the dead body wearing a widow's hat and veil or was her head bare? That would be the clue. If you'd only been paying attention.

Well, there *was* a clue, but you didn't recognize it as one at the time and didn't tell her about it.

You met Flame on the same day you first met the rich widow. Coincidence? You told her the widow's story, she had a different version, seemed to know a lot about it. Or maybe she was just guessing. Making conversation, wanting to make out. You were carrying some pedigree nose candy from Rats, she wanted to share some of it. You were there every couple of nights after that. Eased into the dark by her sultry lullabies. The night they found the body and you first saw that drawing, you dropped by Loui's for a requiem drink and she tried to lure you into staying (Hey, if we are what we eat, baby, I could be you by tomorrow morning . . .), but, still grieving, you went to the Shed instead. Bad choice. She knew that? You were back at Loui's the next night, though, and she was waiting for you. Love? You don't believe in love, victim of it though you too often are, so scratch that. Flame's a working girl. Her job? She tried to tell you a story a few nights ago, but you fell asleep on it. Or were drugged. It was about twin brothers on opposite sides of the law with her in the middle, gun in hand. A gun that went "spat." She seemed to be trying to tell you she was both guilty and innocent of something. Something she couldn't have helped, either way. The cop was using her, but so was the badboy lover. A commonplace tale maybe of love and betrayal, doubled and redoubled, but what you want to know is, who was the cop?

⊙

HEY, BLONDIE'S BACK! FLAME SAYS, GREETING YOU LOV-
ingly when you walk in, opening your pants to take a
peek. Time passes, you say; it's growing out. Her affection seems genuine, but what can you know? Joe pours
you a double on ice, remarking that you smell like you
just crawled out of a sewer, and Loui comes over to
greet you, looking nervous. There's a reward on your
head, dear boy, he says. Lucky for you business has
been good, or I might be tempted.

Yeah, I know, Loui. I've seen the movie posters.
Somebody's trying to pin a bunch of murders on me
and I gotta find out who really did them before I get
grabbed. Starting with that chalk drawing down at the
docks.

You mean, the dead widow?

I was just down there, Loui. Sprang Rats, what
was left of him after Blue's goons had worked him over,
and dropped him off in safe hands. Passed by where the
body was found. All that's left of the chalk drawing is
a faded smudge of the red pubic patch. Should have
paid more attention to that. That was you, wasn't it,
Flame? The artist's model.

Blue's undercover agent stares coolly at you a
moment. She's not as pretty as she was before. She

sticks a cigarette in her mouth and Joe reaches over the bar with a lighter. I owed Blue a favor, she says.

Pretty big favor, sweetheart. Did you also model for the dog-fuck?

Sure, baby. Did you like it?

Who was the dog?

Your friend Blue. He put on a costume. Actually it was a bearskin, only thing they could find. The artist took some liberties.

So did you, sweetheart. Pour me another, Joe.

Blue's after your pretty tattooed ass, lover. I figured if I played along I could buy you some time. She moves in between your legs. I love you, baby. Couldn't let anything happen to you. It's why I bought you that key to the smugglers' passage.

Yeah? Who from?

Don't ask. The price was high. But Blue doesn't know about that. If he finds out, you can come looking for *my* body. She presses closer, whispers huskily in your ear: You'll know it when you see it, Phil. The one with the red patch.

You glance up at the clock over the bar with its tuxedoed rumpot and windmill arms. You wonder how long you were down in the tunnels and ask Joe what day it is. Turns out it's the day you booked the meeting with Snark at the Star Diner. That clock, like all bar clocks, always runs fifteen minutes fast, you can just make it. Got a date, you say, and down your drink, take her hand out of your pants and swivel away, but give her silky ass a farewell stroke (why not, feels good), then hit the streets again.

⊙

IT'S A PERFECT NIGHT. WIND, RAIN, GLOOMILY OVERCAST, the puddled reflections more luminous than the street-lamps they reflect. Cars and buses crash heedlessly through the puddles, forcing you against the wet buildings and blue-lit window displays. You're sucking on a fag, hands in your trenchcoat pockets, your posterboy face hidden behind the upturned collar, thinking about Flame's betrayal, if it was one, about Blue's dark machinations, the mysterious widow, her unknown whereabouts, about all the bodies you've left in your wake. Your tattoo is itching. You reach back under your coat to scratch it with your middle finger erect, just to let whoever's behind you know that you know. What's Blue up to? Maybe he's in Mister Big's pocket, the chalk drawing part of an elaborate cover-up of a heartless murder. Thus the rush to hide the body. Blue figured he could scare you off the case, underestimating your obstinacy, your restless need to know, and what the widow had come to mean to you. Or was he using that obstinacy for some covert purpose of his own?

And is Snark a pal or Blue's agent, his underling and co-conspirator, sending you off on wild goose chases and setting you up to take the fall for others' crimes? If so, whose? Blue's? His and Mister Big's? But why would the big man want to waste a smalltime ivories tickler like Fingers? Because he sent you to an ice cream parlor? Maybe. Message: Helping Noir is not good for your health. Correspondence by cadaver. Body bulletins. You hope Cueball is okay. But why shouldn't he be? Why does it matter? To anyone? Nothing seems to make sense, but why do you expect it to? Shouldn't you just take Mister Big's dream warning to heart and stop trying to figure something out when there is nothing to figure? You glance up at a third-floor window over a drug store where shadows play against a drawn blind. Looks like some guy stabbing a woman. But what can you know? And why (though it will do no good, you stop at a phone booth, call the cops, give them the drugstore address, hang up before they can ask any questions) do you want to? Because the body has to eat and drink so it can stay healthy long enough to enjoy an agonizing death, and the mind, to help out, has to know where the provisions are and how to get them and who else is after them and how to kill them. Then, once it gets started, it can't stop. Gotta know, gotta know. It's a genetic malignancy. Ultimately terminal. Blanche, who reads the Sunday papers, calls it the drama of cognition, or sometimes the melodrama of cognition, which means it's a kind of entertainment. Solving crimes as another game to play; conk tickling, not to let it go dead on you. Murder providing a cleaner game than most. You start with something real. A body. Unless someone steals it. Is that what happened? Who would want it? And what for? Blackmail? Or did Rats snatch it to use as a stash bag? Happened on his turf. Is that why he was nabbed? But why that one in particular? There are bodies all over the city. Up over that drug store, for example. It's a deranged town. A lot of guns but few brains, as someone has said. Did the widow have one in her little purse? Probably. Nested amid the bankrolls. Did she ever use it? If she had one, she probably used it. Put a heater in someone's hands and it's too much fun to pull the trigger and watch your target's knees buckle. Did she use it on her ex? It's possible. What isn't? Taxis pass, their wipers flapping, but they all seem to be driven by guys in leather jackets with goatees and granny glasses. Can't take risks, not enough time for that, must get to Snark, hoping only it's not a trap. Blue could be waiting. But you and Snark have done each other enough favors through the years to create a kind of mutual dependency and you figure Snark will want to preserve that. You squeeze the widow's veil in your pocket for luck, then remember you don't have it anymore. Must be something else.

But though you're hurrying along, running against the clock, it seems to take forever. Everything's stretching out. The blocks are longer somehow, the soaked streets wider and packed bumper to bumper with blaring traffic. You have to double back, take shortcuts that aren't short. You know the way and you don't know the way. You find yourself on unfamiliar corners, have to guess which turn to take. Racing across a street at the risk of having your legs severed at the knees by clashing bumpers, you catch a glimpse of the pale blue police building glowing faintly in the wet night. You shouldn't be able to see it from here, but you do. The city can be like that sometimes. Especially when you're dead on your feet and in bad need of a drink. Joe has a story about it which he regaled you with one day over his ginger ale. This was in the afternoon before happy hour—what Joe calls feeding time at the zoo—so Loui's was quiet. Serene. You were in mourning, not just for the widow, but for Fingers, too, so the atmosphere was right and you had more than one. More than three in fact, who was counting. Joe was not always a teetotaler, and when you asked him why he gave it up, he told you about the night the city turned ugly and nearly did him in. I know you love her, he said. But watch out. She's big trouble. Flame, as you recall, was rehearsing a song in the background, something about a stone-hearted bitch who drives her lovers mad, in which hysteria was made to rhyme with marry ya and bury ya, but later she came over and asked why you two always called the city "she." Well, we're guys, said Joe. That's the way we talk.

⊙

THIS HAPPENED A LONG TIME AGO, BACK IN MY FALL-down-drunk days. I was living on the street mostly, if you could call it living, working as a bouncer, doorman, dealer, garbage collector, barman, pimp, any way to scramble together enough skins for the dog juice. Sometimes I woke up in a hooker's bed, sometimes in an abandoned lot or a back alley, bruised and bleeding but with no memory of the punch-up, if that was what had happened. Now and then I found myself flying with the snowbirds, but mostly I stuck with the hooch. I was sick a lot of the time but sometimes I felt good, and whenever I felt good I got noisy. Sometimes the cops would take me in as a public nuisance, needing someone to pound on for awhile, but usually they let me be, doing nothing worse than push my face into my own vomit, steal my stash, or kick me into the gutter if I was blocking the sidewalk.

It was a shitty life and I began blaming it all on the city. Alkies are like that: everybody's fault but their own. So whenever I got really juiced, I'd start railing crazily at her, calling her every dirty name I could think of at the top of my voice so everyone would know. She retaliated, seemed to, by moving the streets around. Nothing stayed in the same place, that was my impression. When I was sleeping one off, I could hear the buildings walking around, changing places. I didn't know where I was most of the time. Of course, I was also completely scorched most of the time, so I couldn't be sure what was real and what wasn't, though in a sense it was all real, because even if I was only imagining it, it was still real, at least in my own mind, the only one I've got. Which back then I was doing my best to burn to a cinder.

Then one night I stumbled over a loosened manhole cover and fell and skinned my nose and that threw me into a violent rage and I started screaming at her from there where I was lying. You did that on purpose! I yelled. There were noxious vapors belching out of the hole with the loose cover, so, along with all the other filthy things I called her, I cursed her out as a fucking steaming bottomless cunt, and as soon as I said that, I knew I had the hots for her, and I knew she was hot for me. That sounds crazy, it *was* crazy, *I* was crazy, I've said that. But I had to have her and I knew she wanted it. It was all I could think about, to the extent that I could think about anything at all. Come and get me, big boy. I seemed to hear her say that. But how do you fuck a city? The only thing I could come up with was to jerk off over a subway entrance, but when I tried to do that it just made her madder. Maybe she felt insulted or demeaned or just not satisfied, but after that she really got vicious. Mean streets? Until then I had no idea. What before had been a kind of subtle sleight of hand became more like an out-of-control merry-go-round. Whenever I stood up, I got knocked down again. The streets and sidewalks buckled and rolled like a storm at sea, pitched me around, reared up and smacked me in the face. Who knows, maybe I was driving her wild with desire and those were just love commotions of a kind, but they were killing me and I no longer had amorous ambitions. Stroking her while I was down seemed to help, but whenever I tried to stand, she started in on me again. Ever get hit by a runaway building? You don't want that to happen to you. That's when I knew I had to get off the sauce. Until the mob insisted on reinforced steel, Loui used to have a pebbled glass door out there. I got thrown through it. The little fat man took me in and saved my life. Gave me a flop at the back, dried me out. I haven't stepped outside this place since.

SNARK IS WAITING FOR YOU AT THE STAR DINER WHEN you finally find your way there. Snark is depressed and drinking even more heavily than usual from the milk dispenser. His contortionist wife has developed lumbago and all she can do now is knot her arms behind her head and lace her toes, but the more useful middle part is stiff as a board. The Siamese twins got into a fight when one of them tried to run away from home and now they won't speak to each other. They keep trying to turn their backs on each other, but they can't quite, and that's making them hard to live with. Also he's in trouble down at the station because a prisoner has escaped, which in turn has led to a citywide crisis of stoned police officers and Blue is holding him responsible. The bags of shit just turned up in the holding cell when the prisoner crushed out, Snark says. Almost like that was what he was really made of and the spell wore off. Next thing you know: junkie cops. You figure this is Snark's way of letting you know what his cover story is, for you're pretty sure his extra ace was a diversionary tactic to help you out. He has also snuck out your fedora and your old .22. When the prisoner took a flyer, he says, some of the evidence disappeared, too.

Thanks, Snark. You're a pal. Milk's on me. He clinks his mug on yours, drains it, asks the pimply kid behind the counter to squeeze the tit again. Does taste good. That damned Bordox nearly killed you, this is the real thing. Your stomach is comforted by the familiarity of it. You check the inside hatband, which you often use as a crib sheet and reminders list. Or somebody does. Blanche maybe. Sometimes it says things like *Comb your hair*, or *Button up your fly*. Now it says *Cherchez la monnaie.* That sounds like Blanche. Also: *You already know everything.* Who put that there? Your initials are stenciled on the band at the back: PMN. A graffiti artist has circled the M and scribbled *Meathead* above it. One of Snark's semiliterate buddies on the force no doubt, if not Blue himself. When, years ago, you told Snark what it actually stood for, he said you were in luck, with a name like that you'd never grow old. At the time you thought he meant you'd always be young; just as likely, though, he meant you wouldn't last that long.

The panhandler is back, puffy nose flattened against the plateglass window, white hair and beard wet and stringy from the drizzle, watery blue eyes afloat in his gaunt face, staring hauntingly in at you. Not tonight. No more fucking blows to the belfry.

We know a bit more about that rube who got rubbed out with your .22 in the alley, Snark says, signaling for another refill. Seems he came from a small rural community and had a sister in the city, whom he was either trying to kill or was trying to protect, it's not clear. Maybe both.

How'd you learn that?

Some broad called it in. Blue said it looked like a mugging. The guy's coat pockets had been rifled, turned inside out.

That's right. I forgot. I did that on the back stairs. You search woozily for your trenchcoat pockets which keep moving around and, when you find them, reach in and pull out a few scraps of paper, a photo, an all-day sucker, some kid's underpants. Hey, look.

You better get rid of those.

But wait, don't you see, it could have been the fucking Hammer who stuffed that bus station locker I tipped you about.

Yeah, maybe, but how you gonna prove it now he's napoo? Blue has you ticketed for the hot seat, Noir. You're the last person to have seen a lot of people still ticking. At least five, though Blue may think of more. The piano player, the whore at the Dead End, the pervert down at the meat locker, the ape in the alley, the rich jailbait . . .

He doesn't think I killed the widow?

Snark's eyes lose focus for a moment as if in confusion or maybe he's only working up a fart. Oh right. The widow. Six. So all he needs now is evidence you been in some little kid's pants.

You shrug (knowledge: lighter than air; you can just blow it away), tell him to take the drawers home with him, cut an extra leghole in them and see if they fit the twins, and you poke blearily through the other stuff. There's a city map with pier four marked on it, a pawn ticket, a clipping of one of your toy soldier ads, a prescription for painkillers, a lucky rabbit's foot, and a bent black-and-white photo. It's a younger Hammer sitting

on the edge of what could be a park bandstand with a
shit-eating grin on his mush and some doozie standing
behind him, only her southern hemisphere in the photo.

Who's the Jane with the classy shanks?

Don't know. You study the legs, trying to keep
your eyes from crossing. Those beautiful calves. The
widow a few years back? The camera angle from below
allows a glimpse up her skirt into the shadows past her
dimpled knees. The Hammer has his hand up there
behind the legs somewhere. Instinctively, you turn the
photo over to look at her backside, and see written
there: *Today is already yesterday.* You feel a certain
heartache. Or maybe it's just the chili soup. Your head's
spinning. You need some air. Anyway, Snark's gone, you
don't remember when. He was complaining about having to give up pretzels for cold toast and filling his mug
again and then he wasn't there anymore. You unload a
few bills for the night's repast (can't count them, the kid
behind the counter seems happy enough, not yours anyway) and buy a caramel-frosted strawberry and pepper-
corn doughnut for the old panhandler, don your
reclaimed lid and head out into the night.

ONE THING YOU'VE DETERMINED NOT TO DO TONIGHT IS
follow the panhandler on his dark drizzly route, but

that is what you are doing. Trenchcoat collar turned up, fedora brim tipped toward your nose, a wet fag in your mouth, your fried head a bundle of confusions. You sidle along walls to be sure no one's behind you, doing a sequence of spiraling 360s when crossing streets, which probably gives the impression of being staggering drunk, which you are. Blitzed. Smoked. Damn that bottomless Snark. The panhandler continues on his rounds oblivious to your boozy dance behind him, clutching his frosted doughnut. Looking for a bin to put it in maybe; trade it in for some brown lettuce or an old sock. Except for his lifting and lowering of trashcan lids, his soggy shuffle and yours are all that can be heard in the dense clammy night. The tattoo on your butt is itching but that may be because, with all your looping turns, you are in effect following yourself.

No light but for the dull yellow puddles spilled by streetlamps, the cheap rainbow glitter under stuttering neon signs advertising refuges long since shut down. Even when the sun is allegedly out, it never seems to reach back into these claustrophobic back streets, your streets, where you've so long plied your trade that sunnier ones now seem alien to you. You used to spend a lot of time, even when not on a case, chasing the black seam on the back of women's stockinged legs through these streets, these streets and any others where they might lead you. Sometimes up creaky unswept stairwells into sad little adventures that rarely ended well. That was back when you were young and everything was interesting. Some days you would be so focused that all but the legs would disappear, and then they'd be gone, too, just the black seams scissoring along. When you told Blanche about this and asked if you were going crazy, she said, no, you were just a foolish man pursuing your perverse and wayward dreams, an occupational hazard that could lead to a bad ending and jeopardize your career. She recommended that, whenever it started to happen, you should stop in the nearest cafeteria and have a glass of warm milk. You told her you always drank a lot of milk at the Star Diner and it didn't seem to do any good. Blanche's stockings, you assumed, were probably woolly and seamless, but you never looked.

One day, when the seams scissored around a corner and you chased after, you crashed into the dolly who had been sporting them. You have been following me, she said, as though solving a case.

It's my job, lady, you said back, picking yourself up and brushing yourself off. Private eye.

Has someone hired you to do this, Mr. Eye?

Noir, ma'am. No, just practicing as you might say. Keeping my hand in.

Your hand in where?

Wherever I can keep it warm.

But why me, Private Noir?

Just call me Phil, sister. What can I say? I like your legs.

My legs?

That's right, sweetheart. Both of them. And everything in between.

Best you could remember, you'd never said these words before, but it felt like you had. Some kind of catechism, learned before learning. So when she shrugged and said all right, Mr. Sister, I see, if that's what you want, and started taking off her clothes, you were not entirely surprised. This was happening at a busy intersection, the sun doing its strange blazing thing, with café tables set out on the sidewalk like in moviehouse travelogues of island resorts. She stepped out of her underpants and stretched out on one of the tables like the dish of the day. She was gorgeous, the girl of your dreams, and you knew you were suddenly and crazily in love, but out here in the middle of traffic and pedestrians, you weren't sure you could penetrate whipped cream. Worse, you feared that's what it would feel like. Something airy and not quite there. But, hey, life's a mystery, what the hell. You dropped your pants and Blue, chancing by, arrested you for indecent exposure. Wait a minute, what about her? you asked, but the dame had vanished, taking her clothes with her. You seemed to remember her perfect butt, flashing in the sunshine (it had already started to rain again), but maybe you just made that part up in your head and then went on believing it, the way that hoods and killers make up their innocence and never after doubt it. Blue was still slapping you around when Blanche turned up with the bail money and a habeas corpus writ and what you wanted to know was why it took her so long.

WHILE YOU'VE BEEN AROUSING YOURSELF WITH THESE technicolor reveries, you have lost sight of the old panhandler. Maybe one of your 360s was only a 180. You pick yourself up from the running gutter where you've fallen and stumble into a doorway's shadow, head spinning from your drunken revolutions, and consider your options. Also your fate. You consider your fate. It has a flophouse look about it. You take the folded handkerchief out of your lapel pocket and blow your nose in it. Fuck it, you think. You're getting too old for this shit. Back to the office. The sofa. A friendly bottle to suck. Sanctuary. You step out, step back again. Police car. Rolling through the watery street, light wheeling. But in dead silence. As if floating an inch or two above the puddles. No, that's right, can't go back to the office. Blue will have it staked out. What's that sonuvabitch up to anyway? Did he invent a body and send you off chasing phantoms, just to land you in trouble? Probably.

But then what really happened to the widow? Or her remains? You wish you could talk to her again. She was afraid, seemed drawn to you. You were so slow to apprehend. Yet any move you made got you nowhere. And what does all of this have to do with Mister Big? Her dead hubby's partner. His murderer maybe. Hers. And Blue: does he, like everybody else in this fucked-up city, work for Big? Big knows you're after him, so Blue gets sent to nail your ass. But then, Blue has always been out to nail your ass. *Is* Blue Mister Big himself? Your head is aching with these insane ideas. Should just get the hell out of this pestilential hellhole, disappear into some primeval forest somewhere. But what would you do there except die? Sweating like a sick pig in your woolly pinstripes and spotted tie. No, no way out of here, not for you, mister sister. You were born in the city and are destined to live out your life in it. What's left of it. Too little, you suppose. When you told the story in Loui's that night of the crazy broad on the sidewalk café table, Joe the bartender said, yeah, he knew the twist, she's happened to a lot of mugs, and so far as he ever heard, it always ends the same way. Dangerous dame. Scary. So, what would you do if she and her black seams turned up again? Same goddamned thing.

You don't have to go on chasing the panhandler, though. You gave him the doughnut, he gummed a bite, told you a story, and shambled off, you on his tail as though you had no choice. Now you've lost him. Good. You're free. So what next? You can smell the waterfront. You could follow your nose and hole out in a back room at Skipper's. But before you can lean out in that general direction, the old panhandler shuffles by like a silent rerun, bearded chin on his sunken chest, long white hair cascading down past his face and over his shoulders, rainwater dripping from his tattered fedora brim. He clutches his plastic bag to his sunken midriff with both arms, his topcoat tails dragging through the wet street. You lose him momentarily when he turns a corner, and when you catch up to him, he is dead. Sprawled in front of an open bin, strangled, his milky blue eyes glazed and popping. A dirty yellow necktie with purple polkadots knotted around his scrawny throat. You used to have a tie like that, but Blanche made you throw it away. When you gave him the doughnut tonight, he replied as usual with a story. They was this lady walkin' backwards wavin' at somebody and dropped down a manhole, he said. She never come back up and nobody seen it but me, so I reckon she's down there still. He stared up at you. That's purty funny, mister. And you ain't even grinnin'. He spat in disgust past the tooth in his mouth and walked away. Now you wish you'd laughed at his story, cheered the old fellow up once more before he bought it. If you'd not been so blotto, you might have. Reminded you of the old joke: Watch out for the cliff! What cli-i-i-i-if-ff-ff . . . ? Worth at least a nod and a grimace, and you let him down. But what does it matter? Dead's dead, no residue, all's as if it never was. The oldtimer is still clutching the doughnut with the half circle gummed out of it. Not to waste it, you pry it out of his grip and take a bite. As you do, you get a whiff of that special fragrance. Can't place it. But you know what comes next.

No dream this time. Unless you count the thought you had in the split second between fragrance and blow, which you seemed to go on thinking after being sapped: in short, that the city was as bounded as a gameboard, no place to hide in it, no way but one to leave it, you alone and defenseless in it, your moves not even your own. Not much of a thought. A split second was more than enough time for it.

You come around with a half-chewed bite of peppery doughnut in your jaws and a busted head. You know where you are without opening your eyes. Call it a private dick's hunch. There will be glass cases full of toy soldiers and a pedicurist's chair. Welcome, Mr. Noir, says a voice. They said you wished to see me.

Not they, you say. She. When you open your eyes, you'll finally see Mister Big. You're not sure you *want* to see Mister Big. You are mad as hell. At him, at the dead widow who got you into this, at the sick city, sick world, your own meaningless fucked-up life. Your head hurts so, you almost can't think. You'd like to kill somebody. A client, you add bitterly, spitting dough-nut. Late lamented. Whose corpus delicti has gone missing. How do you explain that?

I have no idea, Mr. Noir. Is this a riddle?

Yeah. And the answer is murder. You open your eyes to see at last Mister Big himself. But: not himself. Yourself. You're Mister Big. Gazing at you from across the room. You refuse to be surprised by anything. But you're surprised. Mister Big looks surprised, too. You thought (whiff of cigar smoke?) you caught a glimpse, out of the corner of your eye, of Fat Agnes in his white linen suit fleeing the scene. By way of the window. Right through the heavy drawn curtains as if they weren't there. Maybe they aren't there. Maybe this is the dream you didn't have.

In that case, you would seem to be the answer's answer, says Mister Big; your other you over there. Looking surly. They tell me you've been on something of a spree. He speaks without moving his lips, tough-guy style. You yourself talk that way. Why do you dicks all have that granite look? a client once asked you. Do you take injections? Not only have you apparently done away with a lot of people, he says, but you're also wanted as a thief, pederast, trafficker, and counterfeiter. The sonuvabitch looks sicker than you expected. He's wearing a crushed fedora down over his ears. Ugly scowl on his unshaved pan, doughnut crumbs on his chin. He has stolen your chili-stained tie. There's a twitchy flat-faced mug with a gat standing behind him, and behind the mug a painted hide of some kind in a carved wooden frame. You have the feeling there's a mug behind you. Also twitchy. It's like looking in a mirror. Wait a minute. You see now the backwards "4" on the hide. You *are* looking in a mirror.

Mister Big steps out from behind it. Stringy white hair and beard, watery blue eyes, old pants held up with a sashweight cord: the panhandler. There's something wrong about this, but your head hurts too much to think what it is. They was this here feller come round, he says, lookin' for a body. What's wrong with the one you got? I ast. The feller laughed him a nasty laugh, and says, it ain't got what I need right now, y'ole coot. He was a feller liked to talk mean and live hard and I seen he was headin' for a bad end. His beezer was broke in so many places, if somebody'd tole him to folla his nose, he wouldn'ta knowed which way to go. He was carryin' a filthy darkness round insida him like a canker and he was a chump for the femmes. He talked hardboiled but was really a soft egg and easy to crack. And what mostly made that feller a loser was he didn't want nuthin' bad enough.

You recognize now the twitchy thug with the punched-in kisser in the mirror, the one behind you with the popper pointed at your hatband. The taxi driver. Fingers' ugly sideman. Pug. The .22 he's holding could be yours. Things are beginning to fall into place. On the wall behind him, behind you, Michiko's flayed hide, spread out like a mercator projection, is emitting its own messages, as if making a last effort to help Phil-san. Not easy to read. Besides the mirrored "4," only the equator (the raccoon-dog, the bull's eye) is at all legible from where you sit. That whiff of cigar smoke earlier: probably just stale body powder. You can smell it now. Maybe that *is* the message. If you wept, you might weep for Michiko, but what the hell, it's not the worst end. Everyone croaks. The rest of us end up ash, she's a work of art. It's a glitzy joint with a lot of fat furniture, mahogany tables, framed paint blotches on the walls, layers of exotic rugs, figurines on the fire-place mantel, vases, pots of flowers, and glass cases full of toy soldiers. You recognize the ones you pho-tographed. Maybe the ones. Maybe not. What do you know? If Blanche were here, she could tell you. But the light's odd. Striped as if coming through venetian blinds. But there are no venetian blinds. Hard to focus on anything. The old scarecrow of a panhandler, as out of place in here as a ketchup stain on a tuxedo shirt—or a pearl onion on a banana split, as someone has said—seems sliced up by the light, coming apart and reassembling himself as he shuffles through it.

I tole him they was plenny a live ones out there lookin' for a sweetie, why was he chasin' a dead one? She paid me, he says, showin' how dumb he was, I owe her. Mostly, though, on accounta somebody don't want me to. Well, sonny, says I, if that somebody's who I spose it is, you'll be beddin' down tonight in cold mud.

All the fleabags and flophouses I've bunked in, you say now, cold mud would be an upgrade. How about a fag?

There's a brief hesitation. The old panhandler lifts his head up off his chest for a moment in what might be a nod, and as Pug reaches down with a lit cigarette, you grab the .22, wrest it away, and bust him in the chops with it, turn it on the panhandler. Who is there and not there, drifting in and out of the ribboned light. Pug is snarling at your feet. You point the gun between his eyes. His snarl turns to a high-pitched whimper. You tell him to beat it. On the double. He's out of there on all fours. Tough guy. You throw the bolt on the door. You're alone with Mister Big.

From somewhere, but not necessarily where the panhandler is, or isn't, a voice says: There are at least a hundred men in the building, Noir. You'll never get away.

Maybe getting away isn't the big deal it used to be, pal. We got something to sort out between us. There was this sweet country kid with a rocky past. Abusive father, garbage head for a mother. Came into the city, looking for a fresh start in life, got involved with you and her hubby, got a fresh death instead.

Hard to get a bead on the drifting panhandler. Sonuvabitch never stays in the same place. In some part of your coshed brain, you understand this. And you remember what is wrong. The last time you saw the panhandler, he was dead.

She came to me, you say, picking up the lit soldier on the floor not to waste it and tucking it into the corner of your mouth, because she figured you had brought an end to your business relations with her husband the way a butcher ends his relationship with a pig, and she was afraid it might be her turn to get suicided next. When I took up her case, you turned your stooge Blue on me and had him trump up a lot of phony charges and you even conned her vulnerable kid brother into trying to get rid of me, then bumped him off when he blew it.

The panhandler has paused over near the fireplace where he's poking about in it as if it were a trashbin. You fire a shot, shattering what turns out to be a mirror, and the fireplace disappears, revealing a billiard table behind it, the panhandler shuffling toward it. The fireplace is now seen to be opposite from where you thought it was. Maybe. Your reflection across from you looks confused. You straighten it up, switch on the hard guy again, take a drag, the butt dangling in your lips, smoke curling through your sinuses like a house burglar.

But when you iced my client, you say, something went wrong, and you had to hide the body. You stole it out of the morgue before I could get there. Now, I want that body.

Well, says the voice. The panhandler, over at the billiard table, is putting the balls into a plastic shopping bag in exchange for some rotten oranges and melon rinds. If you insist.

A shot rings out, the .22 flies from your hand, and blood appears there on the trigger finger. It's the widow. She fires again and your hat flies off. There is a lady in the room, Mr. Noir, she says.

Yeah, well, I never was one for the niceties, you gasp, clutching your wounded hand, trying not to cry. I've been chasing a body around. Thought it was you.

It was. I wasn't dead, is all.

So that's how you disappeared from the morgue.

That's right. I walked out. The morgue attendant

tried to tell you that in his vulgar way, sealing his own fate, I'm sorry to say.

You remember this, the odd thing he said. So, you've known all along. Just weren't conscious of your knowing. As she moves around through the harsh rhomboids of glare and shadow (the panhandler has vanished), she multiplies herself in the mirrors. You're surrounded by black-veiled widows, scissored by striped light. Some of them are pointing the gun at you, some are aimed in other directions, which tells you something about which one's the real one, but you're tired now and don't really want to think about it. Who knows, maybe they're all real. Had you pegged from the start, sweetheart, you say, wrapping your bloodied finger in your lapel pocket handkerchief. A gold-digger working the street who struck on a john who wanted to knock off his rich wife. In collusion with your emasculated hometown pimp and your sinister old man, you supplied the murder weapon out of the family drug store in exchange for a marriage contract and a share of the loot. The old story.

But how did you—?

Elementary, lady. Even my office assistant figured that much out.

Your office assistant?

Yeah, Blanche. She's a good kid but no pro at the sleuthing game. Bit of a dummy really but she makes good coffee. The mirrored widows rotate and different ones are pointing at you now. You discovered your husband had taken out a big insurance policy on you, suggesting he did not have in mind an old age together, so you moved first, drugged him and shot him. Like most dames, though, you can't tell right from left and botched it, and there had to be a cover-up. You needed this bigtime racketeer here with his cop and city connections, so you partnered up with him, which also solved the problem of your ex pitting the two of you against each other with his pernicious will. The idea was to hitch up so you could inherit the estate intact, that's where that big rock comes from, not from your deceased dearly beloved, but since neither of you were the type to make do with only half, it was unlikely you'd both live out the honeymoon. Mourning suddenly dead spouses is a weekend sport in your crowd. So you both started making moves. Meanwhile—it's all coming to you now, you feel a certain exhilaration, you're really good at this—your brother butted in, tried to get a piece of the action, you had your psycho pimp and old man take him out. Ugly back-alley stuff. Your dopey hotpants stepdaughter knew too much and had a loose mouth, so you silenced her, too. So far, except for the sex kitten, I haven't mentioned anybody who wasn't also one of your lovers, and who knows, maybe you'd got your talons in her, too. You're a hot ticket and have a lot of poor suckers on the string.

And what about you, Mr. Noir? Are you on my string?

You got classy gams, baby, but I'm on nobody's string. Besides, your lovers all end up in cold storage. Your current stud and business partner hiding behind these mirrors is next whether he knows it or not. It was why you hired me. To try to get a fix on him so you could send in your assassins. You knew the kind of ruthless sonuvabitch you'd signed up with and figured you wouldn't be walking away from your next trip to the morgue, unless you nailed him first and went there for a goodbye kiss. My guess is, you press on, only one of you will walk out of here alive today.

You don't know how much Mister Big is on to all this, but it never hurts to sow a little distrust. She turns as a page might turn and seems to disappear and for a moment you're alone with your reflection. But then she reappears in the mirrored image behind you, the gun pointed at your head. You've got the right kind of trenchcoat, Mr. Noir, but other than that you're a rotten detective. A blind Eye. You deserve to die. You hear the click of the safety and figure you're a goner, but it's your mirrored image across the way that shatters. You're flat on your ass again, pratfelled by fear. Though of course you are fearless. You do what you can, from your some-what awkward position, to show this. You can hear her breathing serenely above you. That and the blood pounding in your ears is all you can hear. You can smell something though. That familiar aroma. The one that drifted up your nose each time you got kayoed when tailing the panhandler. A fragrance you have smelled almost every day and should have paid more attention to.

Blanche!

That was not a nice thing you said about me, Mr. Noir.

Yeah, well, ah, I was only trying to get your dander up, Blanche. I knew all along it was you but I wanted you to give yourself away.

Really? You are so brilliant, Mr. Noir. You take my breath away.

A lotta years in the biz, kid, you say, ignoring her sarcasm. So, lemme see, what's your angle here? You find your fallen fag beside you and, though it's no longer lit, you straighten it out and tuck it back in the corner of your mouth. Helps you think. Blanche just turned up at your office one day and offered her services. When was that? You don't remember. You're not good at that sort of detail. Where did she come from? You never asked. Was the widow's story her own? Was she leading a double life? Was the Hammer her brother, Squeaky her ex-lover? You never thought of Blanche as having lovers. Brothers either, for that matter. You try to imagine her working the streets, picking up a guy with a rich wife, seducing him into murder. You can't imagine it. You realize your deductive powers are being tested, but your appetite for this backstreet knowledge racket is fading. Your stubborn belief that two and two will eventually equal four is probably completely naïve. Some knots, like the twist your thumped brain's in now, cannot be untangled. You have an acute longing for your office sofa. Mister Big probably has a liquor cabinet somewhere, but you're too weary and hurt too much to get off your heinie to go look for it. That damned Blanche can really wield a sapper. Your fedora lies on the floor in front of you with a bullet hole through it. Cherchez la monnaie, she wrote in your hatband. Maybe she was teasing you with a clue. Catch me if you can. So, all right, think about it. There's a fortune to be had and she's going after it. So, it's either the double-life scenario or she knocks the widow off and takes her story on as a kind of second thread. Or maybe the widow's already been snuffed by Mister Big or whomever, and she steps in, puts on the veil, slips into the dead widow's history, hoping to blackmail her ostensible partner into a payoff. One reason to get rid of the body. If there was one. But then along come all those weird family members. Hers or the dead widow's. Something has to be done about them. Something is done about them. By someone. And then there's Blue. He's working for Mister Big. Or for her. You're in the middle. The sucker who gets set up for their crimes. An ignorant grunt at the Battle of Agincourt only looking for a hole to hide in. In your mouse leather brigandine. You explain all this to Blanche who is standing over you. She leans down and lights your crooked cigarette for you. It goes out. She lights it again.

When you sent me into the smugglers' tunnels, that was just a trap.

I didn't send you, it was your friend Flame did that.

Oh. Right. But she's Blue's agent. You may all be in cahoots. What upsets me most is killing my pal Fingers. Just because he tried to warn me.

He was run over. I don't drive, Mr. Noir.

No, that's right. You used a taxi. You and Pug.

Who?

And the morgue attendant. He tries to tell me something about a fake murder and he gets blown away. Sealed his own fate, as you said.

Sorry, but it was your widow friend who said that, Mr. Noir, if I may put it that way. But was it murder? Or was it suicide? He was a man with a fascination for extreme experiences.

Saved the best for last, you mean. Maybe. But what about the poisoned wife, your ex'ed ex, your abusive old man doling out lethal pharmaceuticals, your psycho ex-lover with the squeaky voice?

Oh, Mr. Noir. I just made all that up.

Made it up? Ah. Right. I guessed as much. Made it up. Shit. Didn't I just say so? But who was the guy who attacked me? The Hammer? The guy I saw getting riddled in the alley?

I have no idea. One of Captain Blue's officers? A common thief? I have found, Mr. Noir, that if you make a story with gaps in it, people just step in to fill them up, they can't help themselves.

Your case is coming undone. You've sleuthed up a well-made scenario, several in fact, but your characters are leaving it. You stare at the glowing ash end of your bent butt as though looking for the last word there. You should flick it away, that's always an impressive punctuating gesture, but it's all you've got. But people have died, Blanche, you say, and tuck the smoldering fag back in your lips.

I know. They always do. They won't be missed.

You have to admit, she's one tough cookie. Is she telling the truth? Who knows? As some guy said, when it concerns a dame, does anybody ever really want the facts? Hey, you got great legs, sweetheart, you say, struggling painfully to your feet. Funny I never noticed before.

Sit down, Mr. Noir, she says and fires her gun and the cigarette's not there any more and your lips are burning as when dozing off and smoking a butt to the end and you're back on your ass again. I have some contracts for you to sign. We're going to be partners.

I was just thinking of retiring, you grumble, licking your singed lips.

You can't retire, Mr. Noir. You are wanted for six murders and innumerable other unspeakable crimes. I intend to help you solve all those crimes for Captain Blue and save your life. I'm afraid your choice is between a partnership or what Captain Blue likes to call his electric cure. Now sign here, Mr. Noir, and then let me fix up that finger for you. Luckily, I brought along some iodine.

WHO DO YOU LOVE, BABY? YOU ASK YOURSELF AS YOU walk through the drizzly night streets in your leaky fedora on your way back to the office with black-veiled Blanche, smoking a fag from a fresh pack still reeking of chocolate, rum, and geranium, picked up in the corner drugstore—literally: there was a holdup under way and the owner was somewhat preoccupied, so Blanche plucked a couple of packs off the shelf, gave the money to the holdup man, and led you out before you could play the hero and get into more trouble—and, you reply, silently addressing the dark naked city: You, sweetheart. Joe was right. We were made for each other. Your footsteps echo faintly in the hollow night as if the city were whispering back to you, clucking her tongue, licking her lips.

You'd wanted to celebrate the new partnership with prime rib and a few drinks at Loui's or an in memoriam set at the Shed or at least a five-layer parfait at Big Mame's, but Blanche wouldn't have it, insisting you had to get back to the office before Blue caught up with you. She said she planned to dress you in her widow's weeds until you were out of danger, and this had a certain appeal, but you agreed only so long as you could wear your own underpants. You wondered aloud if Blue was working for Mister Big and she said, no, he was a mostly honest cop. He just doesn't like you is all. As best you can understand it, according to Blanche, she invented a widow and then Blue invented a body, and Blanche borrowed the body idea to move what she is calling the Vanishing Black Widow Caper in a new direction. Something like that.

But wait a minute. What about Fat Agnes?

The ignis fatuus? Just your overactive imagination, Mr. Noir. The risk of pursuing others is that you can also feel pursued. A hazard of the trade, I'm afraid. Rarely fatal but often disabling.

No, come on, Blanche, I *saw* him. He had a little cleft chin and a button nose and thin hair combed across the balding dome. He smoked cigars and wore a fob watch.

So did your father, Mr. Noir.

Ah. Did he? But he seemed so *real*.

You are a sensitive impressionable man, Mr. Noir. And you've taken a lot of blows to the head.

Yeah, right. Thanks for those.

There are other unanswered questions—like, what really happened to the panhandler? is he Mister Big?—but when you broach them, she says: Please. Don't ask. It's all quite simple. But sometimes not knowing is better. It's more interesting.

She's right. You still don't know who did what, but as Blanche has reminded you, that's not really the point. Integrity is. Style. As Fingers liked to say, you can't escape the melody, man, but you can make it your own. You are moving through pools of wet yellow light, surrounded by a velvety darkness as soft as black silk stockings, and it is not the light but the obscurity that is most alluring. The mystery of it. The streets are deserted and, as you turn into them, kissed by the drifting fog, they open up before you, the buildings seeming to lean toward you. Stuttery neon signs wink at you overhead. Behind a steel chainlink fence in an empty playground, a child's swing creaks teasingly. Somewhere there's a melancholic sigh of escaping steam. It's beautiful to be walking down these lush wicked streets with the widow at your side, even if knowing that it's Blanche inside does spoil it a little. Just the same, while she's still dressed as the widow, you wish she'd lift her skirts and show you her legs once more.

You go past a STREET CLOSED sign and find yourself standing in front of your own office building.

Look, says Blanche, lifting her veil and pointing up at the office window on the second floor. BLANCHE ET NOIR, it says. PRIVATE INVESTIGATIONS.

Et, you say. Is that the past tense of eat?

It could be the future tense, Mr. Noir, she says, pushing her horn-rimmed glasses up on her nose and gazing at you under the raised veil with proprietary affection, if you play your cards right.

It's funny. While you're working on a case, every outcome seems possible. When it's over, it's like nothing could have happened otherwise. You are, hand played, where you are. You're not sure whether Blanche is a wannabe private eye or a master criminal, but with a little practice you could get used to her. As long as you have dibs on the office couch. She knows the file system, it's her invention really, she's able to reload the watercooler by herself, and she can sure handle a heater. Your lips are still burning. All right, partner, you say, pursing those tingling lips and popping a little kiss, while lifting and lowering your fedora, deal me in. Her veil drops as though to curtain a blush. But just one more question, you add, looking back over your shoulder. Where the hell have we just come from?

Sorry, Mr. Noir. The Case of the Vanishing Black Widow is closed.